The
Devil's Den

JAMES BABB

Peachtree

Plum Street Publishers, Inc.
LITTLE ROCK

Published 2017 by Plum Street Publishers, Inc.,
2701 Kavanaugh Boulevard, Suite 202, Little Rock, Arkansas 72205
www.plumstreetpublishers.com

Book design by Liz Lester

First Edition
Manufactured in the United States of America
10 9 8 7 6 5 4 3 2 1   HB (ISBN 1–978–1-945268–04–5)
10 9 8 7 6 5 4 3 2 1   PB (ISBN 1–978–1-945268–13–7)

LIBRARY OF CONGRESS CONTROL NUMBER: 2017936127

The paper used in this publication meets the minimum requirements of
the American National Standard for Information Sciences—Permanence
of Paper for Printed Library Materials, ANSI/NISO Z39.48–1992.

Dedicated in memory of my father, Jerry Babb

I did it, Dad.

I did it.

Chapter One

Indian Territory, May 1881

There's a level of anger where a person is just upset, and then there's that dark anger, the kind that boils over and makes people kill. At just fifteen years old, Brody had witnessed both many times, too many times. The Cherokee, Joseph, had been kind to him, had given wise advice as Brody worked for him trapping furs, but now there was nothing but dark anger about the Indian standing before him.

Joseph hunched his wide shoulders as he leaned forward, bringing his battered and swollen face closer. He separated his lips into a snarl. With clenched fists, he towered over Brody, seeming to grow taller and more menacing with each passing second.

The sight reminded Brody of a killer bear, like the one that had torn into his cabin last year, growling with a rabid kind of madness. His voice trembled just a bit when he spoke. "Joe, calm down a little."

Joseph's deep voice thundered through the camp. "No one will stop me from finding my son!" He threw out one hand and pointed. "These are your bullets, Brody! What happened to Todd?"

Brody looked at the four empty rifle cartridges scattered on the ground, then his gaze settled upon the angry Cherokee standing in front of him. A jagged cut on his face was coated in a salve, but the stained bandage on his forearm was seeping blood.

Brody struggled to get his thoughts together. He was astounded that Joseph was alive, but he was here and—by the look on his face—willing to move mountains to get to Todd.

"Answer me," Joseph demanded.

"Joe, it's okay. Todd is okay," Brody said quickly. "When I found him he was in a bad way. That madman that attacked you and Todd, well, it scared him so badly he couldn't talk and took sick. My folks were the only ones I thought could help him."

Brody swallowed hard and struggled to continue. "But Frank and Billy Miller, along with some bounty hunters, came for me. We had already fled with Todd into the woods, but they burned down Momma and Papa's house for pure hate. They would've killed all of us. I had no other choice. I left Todd with my family in Arkansas so I could draw the bounty hunters away. I wanted to wear them down and eventually lose them here in Indian Territory. I didn't know what else to do."

Joseph stood motionless for a long moment. Some of the anger seemed to wash out of him, leaving him stern and determined. "We are going to find my son—and your family." He glared across the fire at the older Indian standing there. "And we are going right now."

When Joseph had first stepped out of the brush and into camp Brody had forgotten about the terrifying man who had threatened him. Now, at least, his ancient bow was down by his side and no longer pointed at Brody.

The old man said something to Joseph. They exchanged a volley of harsh words that were just a garble to Brody's ears.

"What is he saying?"

"My father is old and very cranky."

Brody's eyes grew wide. "This is your father?"

Joseph walked away from them and into the woods. His father raised his voice, shouting in Cherokee.

"What is he saying?" Brody hollered after Joseph, never taking his eyes off of the old man.

Joseph had completely disappeared into the brush, but his words floated out of the woods. "He wants to know if he can kill you now."

"Kill me?" Brody yelped.

He stared with unblinking eyes at the Indian before him. The wispy gray ponytail at the top of his shaved head waved in the May breeze. His dark face was deeply lined, and though this was the oldest Indian Brody had ever seen, his muscles were visible. He looked sturdy for his age. His long, slightly crooked nose looked as if it had been broken in the past. The Cherokee's dark eyes bore into Brody, filling him with dread.

"Do not worry," Joseph said. He emerged from between the tall bushes, leading a big red roan and a smaller white and black spotted horse, both with saddles. "I told him to let you live." He smiled grimly.

Brody stepped closer. "Are you mad at me, Joe?"

After handing the spotted horse's reins to his father, Joseph turned to Brody. His face softened slightly. "I never expected to see you again. I was sure you would flee from these parts forever, but you, Brody Martin, came back and saved my son from a monster. It would be unwise to be upset with you."

Joseph's father slung his bow across his back and leaned on his horse. His stern gaze remained fixed on Brody.

"Are you sure you told him not to kill me?"

Joseph gave a brief nod. "He will not kill you."

Joseph's reassurance did little to settle Brody's nerves. "What is his name?"

Looking to his father, Joseph said, "He refuses to take a Christian name. He is called Wolf Jaw."

"Wolf Jaw," Brody repeated. "He should be called Angry Wolf."

Wolf Jaw was now pointedly ignoring Brody. The Indians Brody had seen in Fort Smith wore clothes that looked like the rest of the folks there, but Wolf Jaw was wearing a deerskin shirt.

His leather leggings and breechcloth were worn and discolored. Old moccasins with leather fringes covered his feet. "Does he understand English?"

"He understands very little," Joseph grumbled. "He does not want to learn. Get your horse, Brody. We must go now."

Brody's stomach growled. "Hold on." He bent down and started cutting up the burnt turkey in the pan by the fire. Joseph pulled himself into the saddle, wincing with pain, and then took the meat Brody held out to him. He also offered Wolf Jaw a drumstick, but the Indian scowled at him and swung up on his horse.

Brody whistled to get Buck's attention. His horse looked at him, his ears pitched forward. Brody gnawed on the turkey leg as he walked across camp to his buckskin. Buck reached out to lip Brody's sleeve until he caught the scent of the cooked meat. He snorted and bobbed his head up and down. Brody picked up the rein dragging the ground and threw it over Buck's neck. He patted the long face of the horse affectionately.

"Easy, boy. You'll get a treat just as soon as I can rustle one up. For now, we got to head out again." With a final pat, he put a foot in the stirrup and swung up.

They trotted the horses down the track with Joseph beside him and Wolf Jaw behind. His mind was spinning after everything that had happened, and he dreaded the decisions he was going to have to make very soon.

He needed to go north and warn Ames. The black man may have been a little touched in the head, but a year ago he had saved Brody's life after a hunting accident. Now Brody counted him as his best friend. He desperately needed to let Ames know that bounty hunters were looking for them, but Joseph was determined to head south when they crossed the river into Fort Smith.

While he pondered on what to do, Brody looked at the cuts on Joseph's skin. He shuddered at the thought of Joseph in the hands of that murderer.

"Will you tell me what happened to you and Todd?" Brody asked

"That monster came in the night. No man has ever caused me fear, but this madman was more animal than man. He growled and slashed at us with that double-bladed weapon. I fought him, and he cut me. I yelled for Todd to hide in the woods. I hoped he would go to the trap line and wait."

"That's close to where I found him," Brody said. "We were stalked and barely made it out."

Joseph continued. "That ugly devil wounded me many times, and we stumbled and fell. We wrestled until I could hardly breathe."

"How did you get away?" Brody asked.

"A lucky blow stunned him long enough for me to run. My blood was flowing too freely, though. I knew he would trail me to a kill and then go after Todd. I tried to lead him as far away as I could."

Brody had become so engrossed in Joseph's story that he forgot to swallow his turkey. "Where did you go? Ames and I looked for a long time but couldn't find you."

"A fever came over me, and I do not remember much after that first night. I woke in the cabin of a Cherokee man that had come across me in the woods. He remembered me from when I was young and sent for my father."

"Then you came back to find Todd," Brody said.

Joseph nodded. "I believed that madman had killed my son. I came back to hunt him down. Now I will find Todd, and then I will come back here and kill that evil man."

"He's already dead, Joseph."

Joseph's eyes widened, and his head snapped toward Brody. "How do you know this?"

"Ames came back with me, and we looked until we found a steel trap set for us. He had stolen hundreds of traps over the years and had them hanging in the trees."

"Hanging in the trees?" Joseph repeated in disbelief.

"He had sharpened them and filed the levers down until they were hair-triggered. We made it through and found where he was living. He had horses, saddles, knives, and all sorts of things he had taken. We found some of your stuff and figured for sure he had killed you."

"How did this devil meet his end?"

"Ames wounded him and we tracked him to a cliff. He jumped out of his hiding place and threw me around like a rag doll. A big trap clamped down on my boot, and the wildman and I went over the edge. He crawled back up the chain and left me hanging upside down." Brody's stomach clenched up as he told the story. He would never forget that horrific day. "He was trying to shake me loose when Ames got ahold of him. They fought until the madman went over the cliff to his death."

"He is dead? Are you sure?" Joseph asked.

"Dead." Brody said. He stared at the cut under Joseph's ear. "I really thought you were dead too."

"Nearly." Joseph kicked the horse's sides, and the red roan broke into a trot. "We need to move faster."

Ahead of them, the crossroad came into view. Brody had waited as long as he could, and now the time he dreaded had come. He pulled back on Buck's reins and said, "I have to go find Ames first."

Chapter Two

Joseph yanked back hard on the reins, making his red horse slide to a halt. Little puffs of dust stirred up from the track.

Wolf Jaw pulled his horse to a stop. The older Indian said something that sounded like a question. Joseph glanced at him and then turned his attention to Brody. "We must find my son."

"I know, but I just can't go with you," Brody said. "My folks will keep Todd safe, but nobody is looking out for Ames. Miller's bounty hunters will find him for sure, and I have to get there first to warn him."

"I. . . ." Joseph paused, then his face hardened. "I cannot wait. We have to get my son first."

"Please," Brody begged. "I have to go warn Ames."

"Todd first," Joseph stated firmly. His voice brooked no argument.

Brody leaned forward. "I can warn Ames without you, then I can come back and catch up with you tomorrow."

Joseph was shaking his head. "We will be riding hard, and you must show us where your family has taken Todd. We cannot find them without you."

"Joe," Brody pleaded, "I know they were going to our old farm, and I can tell you exactly how to get there. That night the Millers set fire to the house, my momma said they would head out to the old farm the next morning."

Joseph cocked his jaw to the side and stared at Brody for a few seconds. "You risked your life for my son. This friend must mean much for you to risk your life again."

"Yes," Brody said quietly.

Joseph shifted restlessly in the saddle. He looked over at his father, then back to Brody. "We will divide our paths if you tell me where to find my son."

Relieved, Brody quickly told him how to locate the old cabin on the farm south of Fort Smith. Joseph nodded as Brody gave directions.

"I can find this place," Joseph said.

Pulling on Buck's reins, Brody started to turn north. "I'll find you as soon as I can."

"Wait," Joseph said forcefully. "Bad men are looking for you. You have said so. I will not let you go alone."

Brody's eyes darted to the old Indian, and he feared what Joseph was going to say.

As Joseph spoke to Wolf Jaw, the old Indian's lip curled as if he had tasted something disgusting. His gaze locked with Brody's as he snarled something in Cherokee.

"'I-chew-a-jaw'? Is that what he's saying? What does it mean?"

"It just means 'boy.'"

"Well, the way he says it kind of gives me the jitters."

"My father will go with you."

"Uh, Joe, I reckon he don't want to." Brody shook his head. "I think I agree with him, too. I can go by myself. I've done it before."

Joseph started shaking his head before Brody was finished speaking. "I do not know what danger my son may be facing, and I cannot be distracted by worry over you."

Joseph spoke to his father again. Wolf Jaw's scowl grew darker. He gestured with his hands while he spoke, spitting the words out as if they were poison. He let out a long string of phrases, repeating 'I-chew-a-jaw' several times.

Brody knew by the man's tone what he was saying, even if he could not understand the words. "I don't think he likes me very much."

"He will go with you, or you will not go." Joseph motioned

at his father. Wolf Jaw muttered under his breath and shot a threatening look at Brody as he kicked his horse hard. They shouldered into Buck, who laced his ears back and reached out to bite the offender's rear.

Brody pulled the reins, rubbing his horse's neck soothingly. Looking at Wolf Jaw's stiff back and then to Joseph, Brody frowned. "Are you sure he won't kill me?"

The old Indian shouted and shook a fist in the air as he walked his horse away from them.

"What did he say?" Brody demanded.

Joseph spoke to his father sharply, but Wolf Jaw ignored him and headed down the road. "He says you killed all the buffalo."

"I've never even seen a—"

"I know." Joseph sighed. "He knows this also. He is just an old man who refuses to let go of the past. He is like a dog gnawing on an old bone. He growls and barks, but he rarely bites."

"I don't want him to go with me. He should be with you, looking for his grandson."

Joseph looked back at Brody. "He has not been part of Todd's life. I hope to change that someday. Allow my father to go with you and protect you."

"Protect me? He's old. How's he going to keep me safe?"

"I need you to do this."

Brody opened his mouth to argue again.

Joseph looked down at his hands clenched tight around the leather reins. "It would be an insult if you refuse. He will not hurt you, and he will watch after you because I told him you are a son to me."

Brody slowly closed his mouth. He could hardly believe Joseph's words. He had brought terrible trouble to this man, and yet Joseph was calling him family.

Without another word, the large man turned his horse and headed down the road.

Brody finally found his voice. "Wait!"

But Joseph didn't wait, and Brody watched him ride away. After a few seconds, he looked over at Wolf Jaw. The old Indian had stopped a little way down the track and was staring back at him with cold piercing eyes.

He picked Buck's reins up and clucked to him. The buckskin quickly caught up to the Indian, and Brody avoided looking at him when he passed by. After he had pulled ahead, he could hear Wolf Jaw's horse coming up behind him. It took all of Brody's willpower to keep from looking back.

The trip into Crawford County was quiet and awkward. The situation reminded him of how he felt when his parents fought. It was rare when they had cross words, but when it did happen it always made Brody feel out of sorts. This old Indian was giving him that same uneasiness—well, that and his threat to kill him.

Over the past year, the road in Brody's life had been a tangled and twisted one. With a starving family threatening to abandon the farm he loved, Brody had gone hunting without telling anyone. The disaster that awaited him had led to an unshakable friendship with a peculiar black man named Ames.

That friendship had led to the death of Billy Miller's brother, Doc, and exposed Billy and his son, Frank, as corrupt landowners who cheated their sharecroppers. Billy had lost his job as a deputy because of the ledgers Brody and Ames had discovered.

The Millers despised them with such a cold venomous hate that Brody could barely comprehend it. Billy had accused them of murder and horse theft, and then tried killing him, burning him out, and when that failed, setting bounty hunters loose on both of them.

Now he was in the company of an old Cherokee who hated white people. He shook his head in wonder over how he had managed to stay alive this long.

Brody couldn't control his anxiousness any longer. "Wolf Jaw, uh . . . I'm just going to call you Wolf. Is that all right?"

The Indian's stare betrayed no emotion whatsoever.

"I know you don't like me." Brody rubbed his saddle horn nervously. "We have to get along though, so I'm going to talk to you and treat you like I would anybody else."

Wolf's expression remained unchanged.

"My name is Brody. Can you say, Brody?"

Instead of offering a reply, Wolf looked down the road and ignored him. Brody was beginning to feel downright silly, but he forged ahead in spite of it.

"See, I met Joseph in Fort Smith and he offered me a job trapping with him and Todd."

At the mention of Todd's name, Wolf glanced at Brody. Encouraged, Brody continued.

"Todd is a great boy, and I treat him like a little brother. My folks didn't have any more kids than me, so having another brother is good. Even though he can sure be a trickster, he is smart and funny. Joe has done a great job raising him even if he isn't teaching him your customs."

They rode in silence for a while, until the tension eased from Brody's shoulders. He watched Wolf out of the corner of his eye. "So, Wolf, why do you think I killed all the buffalo?"

Brody lowered his voice and did his best impression of how he imagined Wolf would sound if he could speak English. "You have that famous rifle with the strange stock. Everyone knows you are a crack shot."

"You mean my Henry rifle? As a matter of fact, it was Joe who suggested I carve a new stock. It is a little rough looking, but it's longer and sets against my shoulder tight when I shoot."

Wolf kept facing forward, offering no indication that he heard anything Brody said.

Brody lowered his voice again. "How did you get that scar on your forehead?"

"This scar?" Brody pointed to the old burn on his face. "I got this because I was careless with some black powder. Nearly blinded me for life. Ames found me in the woods and got me healed up. Anything else you want to say, Wolf?"

"You kill buffalo and now I must kill you."

Brody chuckled at his ridiculous conversation, but stopped abruptly. "I'm not laughing at you, Wolf. I know you can't understand me, but I am truly sorry about the buffalo. I didn't kill any, though, and neither did my father or my grandfather as far as I know. I heard tell there were millions, once. It is hard to believe they are nearly gone."

Wolf looked at him and spat on the road between the horses. All of Brody's silliness left him, and his nervousness was back in full force. He leaned over his saddle and kicked Buck into a gallop. Over his shoulder he saw Wolf's pied horse break into a long stride, the old man comfortably settled in the saddle. He kept several paces behind Buck, which was fine by Brody.

After finding a good place to cross the river, they moved into Arkansas and slowed the horses down to a trot. Their journey took them down several winding wagon tracks that alternated between thick woods and blocks of pasture. Shacks and small cabins lined the road in some sections, with sturdy well-built houses set back off the main lane every now and then.

Brody pulled back on Buck's reins, stopping at a crossroad. He pointed down a rugged little track. "Wolf, my friend lives just a ways there. He's a little strange sometimes, but Ames is a good man, so don't try to kill him if he comes out with a gun."

Wolf stopped by Brody. His stern look and permanent scowl gave Brody the chills. Glancing at the old bow across the Indian's back, he noticed Wolf's quiver. It held only four arrows. They were newer than the bow but nowhere close to being straight. The thought crossed his mind that Ames would probably be safe even if Wolf shot all four arrows at him.

As Brody and his Indian escort arrived at a little white-washed home, Brody shouted, "Hello to the house!" A big yellow dog bounded off the front porch, barking loudly.

A middle-aged black woman came out, shushing the dog. It seemed to Brody that Mary had more gray in her hair, but her thin frame had filled out some and her large dark eyes still looked kindly at him.

"Brody!" she called happily as she started down the steps. "Where you been?" Her gaze landed on Wolf, and she stopped short.

Brody jumped down and ran up to hug her. "A lot has happened since I saw you a few weeks ago, Mary."

Mary looked past him, toward Wolf. She whispered, "Brody, why you with that old red man?"

Brody looked back. The Indian was calmly staring off in the distance, ignoring everyone.

"He's Joseph's father. Joe sent him with me. Is Ames here?"

"Luke!" Mary shouted, still keeping an eye on Wolf.

Luke came to the doorway. "Brody! Good to see you." He paused, then pointed at Wolf in amazement. "Hey, who's the Indian?"

"Don't be rude like that, Luke!" Mary chided. "Brody is looking for Amos." She leaned closer to her son-in-law and whispered, "I'll tell you later 'bout the red man."

Mary's daughter stepped outside. Anna's belly had grown, but she still was as pretty and graceful as ever. "Brody Martin, as I live and breathe! It's so good to see you!"

"You too, Anna! When's that baby supposed to be here?"

"Oh, still got some months to go. Luke is so proud you'd think he was the one having him." Anna laughed as her husband ducked his head in embarrassment.

Luke changed the subject. "Say, Brody, if you're a-looking for Amos, he's over in the field. Come on." He started to come off the porch but paused. "What about your . . . um . . . Indian friend?"

They all looked at Wolf. Wolf stared at some point off in the distance. Brody cleared his throat. "Uh, Wolf?" The old Indian didn't bat an eye or turn to look at him. Brody stepped closer and spoke louder. "Wolf Jaw!"

Wolf still did not move. Brody shrugged and turned back to join Luke, walking toward a little hill that rose next to the house. They heard a slow thudding of hooves and looked back to see Wolf following them on his horse.

Mary and Anna waved at them from the porch. "Y'all go on and find Amos," Mary said. "We'll get you a good meal on by the time you get back with him."

Luke tried to talk to the Indian as they walked. "Are you Choctaw or Cherokee?" Wolf stared past him and didn't answer.

"He does not speak English," Brody said. "He's Cherokee."

"He seems awful crotchety," Luke said.

Brody laughed. "You have no idea."

When they topped the hill they faced a large green field just below them. The rolling landscape flowed down from a rocky ridge. Sparse trees dotted the gentle slope, but the land below had been cleared. The field held row upon row of tiny green plants.

"He's over there, toward the back. See him?"

Brody spotted the tall, sturdy black man, bent low, looking at the ground. "Luke, I need to talk to Ames about something. It has to do with the Millers."

Luke's face tightened up. "I thought we was done with them evil men."

Brody shook his head and sighed. "It's probably better to not get involved if you can help it."

Luke looked at him a long moment. Finally, he said, "Anna needed some water drawn up for washing. I best be tending to it."

Brody watched Luke walk back toward the house. He turned to Wolf. "I'm going to talk to Ames. You stay here." He pointed at the ground. "Stay. Don't follow me."

Brody walked between rows of young seedlings just a few

inches tall. Glancing back, he saw Wolf had gotten off his horse and was standing with his bow in one hand, looking out across the field. Brody felt his skin prickle, but after several glances back the old man remained still as stone.

The black man in the straw hat straightened as Brody got closer. Ames still reminded Brody of an old oak tree, sinewy and rough, scarred up by the many storms in his life but strong and tough as a leather hide.

When Brody reached him, Ames leaned on an old hoe. "Well, hey, li'l fella!"

"Hey, yourself, big fella!" Brody grinned. "How's your leg? Still hurting bad?"

"'Bout the same. Did ye see Mary and the kids?"

"I did. Mary said to bring you back and she would have us something to eat." Brody's stomach growled about that time, and they both laughed.

Ames took his straw hat off and wiped the sweat from his forehead. "Seems longer than two weeks since I done seen ye. Come to help work them crops, did ye?"

Brody shook his head. "I need to talk to you, Ames. Joseph is alive."

Ames cocked his head to the side and frowned. "How in the world? We looked. We looked hard, Brody."

"I know. It's a long story, but that's not why I'm here. I came to warn you."

"What got ye worried?"

"The Millers have some bounty hunters looking for us."

Ames's face twisted into a scowl, and his hand tightened on the hoe handle. "Bounty hunters!"

"Billy Miller sent them to track you and me down. They were in Indian Territory, then I lost them."

"I knowed they was a bounty out, but I figured it were over since old Miller found himself in trouble."

Brody picked up a pebble from the freshly turned earth and

rolled it around in his palm. "It's not over by a long shot. Billy has gone mad and swore he would not give up until he got ahold of us."

Tossing the pebble out across the field with all his might, Brody watched its path. "They burnt the farmhouse my folks just moved to, Ames. They burnt it up and nearly killed Daniel."

"Your li'l friend the stable boy?"

"They shot him!" Brody's anger flared up. "The Millers won't stop. Billy has plenty of money to put up a bounty, and those men he hired are nothing but killers."

"They burned your house? Brody, I'm right sorry for such a thing. I reckon your folks made it out?"

Brody nodded. "Momma suspected they would come back for me and had us get out. Papa didn't want to go, said we needed to take a stand. But my momma was right . . . They would have killed all of us, including Todd."

Ames started to get riled. He brought the hoe up and cradled it across his body, like it was a rifle. "She done right. Brody, I'm not liking this one bit."

"I took off for Indian Territory to lead them away from my folks, but I lost them somewhere on the trail. Joseph found me before they did."

"They gonna be coming here next," Ames growled. His eyes focused over Brody's shoulder, and he stiffened.

"They found us!"

Chapter Three

Before Brody could turn, Ames grabbed his arm in a tight grip and took off, hoe still in his other hand. Tripping over his own feet, Brody stumbled, but Ames kept going, dragging him out of the field and into the thick brush by the woods. The big man limped with each running step, but it didn't seem to slow him at all.

"What—what is it?" Brody panted, trying to catch his breath. "The Millers?" He twisted around, trying to get his feet back under him. "Wait, Ames. Let me—"

Ames flung Brody into a thicket and crashed down next to him, swinging the hoe wildly, the metal end barely missing Brody's head. "It's one of them bounty hunters." Brody tried to peek through the brush, but Ames pushed him back down.

"Did he have on a red shirt? That's what one of them wears."

"He are an ugly looking devil." Ames parted the branches slightly and peered through it. He grabbed the hoe again. "Here he come," he said softly.

"I don't have my gun with me!" Brody looked frantically around for anything that would work as a weapon.

"Ain't no other choice," Ames whispered. "We gonna have to run."

He jumped to his feet with surprising agility and took off in a limping run. Brody scrambled up but got tangled in a brush root and plopped over, flat on his back. A face blocked out the sun. Brody flung up his hands to ward off his enemy. He heard a snort of derision, and then the face vanished.

The heavy thud of someone running in boots was growing louder. "Get on back away from him!" Ames shouted.

Realization dawned on Brody. It was Wolf. "No! Stop!" Brody yelled, clawing his way up out of the thicket.

Ames brandished the hoe but had halted about ten feet from Wolf, who had drawn his bow, an arrow already nocked.

Raising his hands, Brody started toward him. "Wait. Wait! Hold on!"

"Get back, Brody!" Ames rushed forward.

Wolf pulled the bowstring tight and sighted down the arrow, shouting fiercely.

Brody stepped between the men and yelled at the top of his lungs. *"No!"* He looked at Ames and flung out a hand at Wolf. "He's not a bounty hunter! Just calm down."

"He gonna shoot us. Get over here!"

"He's not going to shoot us." Brody turned to Wolf. "Put it down." Motioning with his hands, he signaled for Wolf to lower his weapon. Wolf curled his upper lip in a snarl but relaxed the bowstring a bit. Brody nodded and pointed at Ames. "He won't hurt you."

"He will too done it." Ames growled, ready with the hoe cocked back to swing. "He ain't nothing but a dirty old bounty hunter!"

"Put the hoe down, Ames. This is Wolf, Joseph's father. He's not going to shoot us."

"Ye sure this is Joseph's daddy?" Ames did not take his eyes off the Indian.

"Yes!"

"Well, what he doing following ye here?"

Ames and Wolf lowered their weapons slowly. Each stared at the other. Stepping over, Brody pulled the hoe away from Ames and dropped it. "Joseph sent him to watch after me."

"He sure are ugly." Ames wrinkled his face as if it hurt to look at Wolf.

"Ames, listen to me."

"What happen to his hair?"

"He's Cherokee," Brody said. "Are you listening to what I'm saying?"

"He sure are mean and ugly."

Wolf put his arrow away and draped the bow across his shoulder.

"Don't worry about him," Brody said to Ames. "That bow is older than the hills."

"Them arrows as crooked as my leg too."

"Let's go back to the field," Brody said. "Come on." He walked away and waved for Ames and Wolf to follow.

Ames picked up his hoe and followed Brody but kept his distance from Wolf. After they reached the edge of the field, Brody stopped and explained everything again. Ames nodded but kept glancing toward Wolf. The longer Brody talked, the more Ames relaxed. His tense shoulders eased down, and the bulge in his jaw muscles disappeared.

"We can't keep going like this," Brody said. "What if it would have been the bounty hunters? Or the Millers?"

Ames shook his head and sucked air between his teeth. "We gots to end all this, Brody. My family done lived through enough troubles, and they gots a home and land now. It ain't right they gotta go on living scared every day."

"When Joseph and I were trapping, he found out the trouble we were in. He said we should talk to that deputy they call Reeves. He works for Judge Parker in Fort Smith. Joseph tells me he's an honest man."

"No way we should trust the law." Ames snorted. "Billy Miller is a deputy. A deputy for Judge Parker! They all stick together."

"Billy *was* a deputy," Brody said. "Those ledgers proved he was a liar and cheat, and they took his badge."

"What if we get throwed in jail?"

"What if we don't? It's time for this to be over. Billy Miller hates us so bad, he won't ever stop sending killers after us."

Brody mulled over the accident that killed Billy's brother. He could still see Doc Miller charging his horse and buggy toward Ames; Brody had no choice but to shoot. Things had only gotten worse when Brody helped Ames get his family out of their crooked sharecropping contract, and humiliated Billy's son in the process. The ledgers they had taken from Frank's house had gotten the Millers in terrible trouble. It looked like Billy and Frank would stop at nothing to kill them both.

He was losing count of the times the Millers had come after him or Ames, or even those he loved. Each time he encountered a Miller—or even heard the name—that dreadful feeling in the pit of Brody's stomach got bigger and bigger.

Ames took a deep breath, drawing in air long and slow before letting it out. "I don't like it, li'l fella, not one bit. But I reckon we can't stop all them bounty hunters alone. Only look here, I gots to catch us a thief afore we go."

"A what?"

"I were looking for an egg thief when you got here."

Ames pointed to the spot where Brody had found him in the field. "Found tracks and a dropped egg over there when I was working the field. It ain't no chicken snake like we was thinking."

Brody could not keep his frustration at bay. "Ames, we can't hang around here, trying to catch some dang thief stealing eggs while bounty hunters are looking for us!"

The stubborn look on Ames's face was one he had seen many times before. "Can't leave now, we need them eggs to feed us. If them thieves decide to steal out of the field, we go broke."

Looking at the tiny plants, Brody said, "What are they going to take out here? You don't have any vegetables yet."

"We will soon," Ames said. "And we can barely take care of the crops now. If they lock me up, how all this work gonna get done? It would just be Luke and Mary, 'cause Anna gonna be having that grandchild afore long."

"Ames, if we don't do something about Miller and those

bounty hunters, these crops won't matter at all when they show up here."

Ames paused to consider. He glanced over at Wolf. Wolf had folded his arms and was staring across the horizon, oblivious to the whole conversation. His friend turned back to Brody with a troubled face.

"Them thieves been coming every day, and now the tracks done told me which way to watch for them. If we catch them tonight, we can leave in the morning."

"Even if we don't. If we don't catch them, we still have to leave in the morning."

Ames nodded.

"You promise?" Brody asked.

Ames nodded again. "Just don't know how we gonna do crops if I get locked up."

"You got more to worry about than crops. If Billy Miller or the bounty hunters show up here, it's your family you'll be worrying about."

Ames clenched the hoe handle hard. He closed his eyes for a moment, and then opened them. "All right."

Wolf followed them to the house but refused to go inside. Anna and Mary put food on the table while they chatted about the farm, the crops they anticipated, and the coming baby. Luke cast worried glances at Ames and Brody but kept quiet.

Brody went outside and offered Wolf some cornbread and new potatoes, but he shook his head. Brody suspected he had his own food in the leather pouch tied to his saddle.

After eating, Ames wiped his mouth. "We gonna catch them egg stealers tonight."

Mary looked out the window. The sun was casting long shadows across the yard. "You boys be careful. A few missing eggs isn't worth getting hurt over."

"It starts with eggs, and it ends up being our crops and tools!" Ames argued. He picked up his musket from the corner by the door.

Mary shoved a warm package of cornbread and butter in Brody's hands. She lowered her voice. "You keep an eye on him, Brody? You know how he can get."

"Sure, Mary, I'll watch out for him."

"And, Brody, what about your Indian friend out there? You think he needs a place to sleep tonight?" she asked, wincing ever so slightly.

"Oh, I am pretty sure if he won't come in to eat with us, he sure won't come inside to sleep." Brody had to bite back a chuckle at the relief on Mary's face.

"Brody, I'll put your horse with the mules and grain him," Luke said.

"I sure appreciate that, Luke. Just let me get my gun in case we need it tonight."

Brody followed Ames outside in the waning light. They ended up behind the house at a well-built chicken coop. There were hens of all sizes in the fenced-in yard, busily scratching for bugs or drinking out of a heavy pan of water. Some chickens were headed inside by way of a small trap door in the front wall, and a couple of watchful roosters kept an eye on the newcomers.

Ames opened a door in the side of the coop. Several chickens cackled loudly in alarm. "See them laying boxes? We get close to twenty eggs a day. Well, we was until them egg stealers started coming."

"How are we going to catch them?" Brody asked.

Ames glanced over Brody's shoulder and sucked in a quick, startled breath. "Dadgum, ye sneaky red Indian! Brody, he gonna just show up like that, ever time we turn around?"

"Joseph told him to stay with me."

"He don't act like he likes you none."

"I don't think he likes anyone," Brody said. "He says I killed all the buffalo."

"He a crazy man," Ames said.

Brody couldn't stop a chuckle. "You ought to know."

Ames grinned, though a bit sadly. "I been doing better. Working them fields sure puts a man right to sleep at nights. Don't chase no ghosts when ye too tired to pay attention to 'em."

"Glad to hear it, Ames." Brody slapped him on the shoulder. "Bet Mary's really glad, too."

Ames lost his grin at that. He turned away quickly but not before Brody caught a look that made his heart hurt. It seemed that not all his friend's ghosts had been laid to rest.

After leading them to a thick stand of trees, Ames looked for a good place to hide. "They won't see us here," he said.

Between the trunks and brush, Brody could see the coop. "Why don't we hide in the chicken pen?"

"No, sir," Ames warned. "We got some game banties and Rhode Islands in there."

Brody whistled. "I heard about those breeds. My grandpa said those were some of the meanest kinds of chickens to have."

The black man chuckled ruefully. "Well, we sure got 'em cheap when they was chicks. Now they's an awful mess of pecking and spurring. You go in and they gonna get you. Daylight times, no critter can take 'em without getting cut up. Even our yeller hound won't go near 'em."

Ames sat under a towering oak and leaned against its trunk. Brody sat next to him, placing his gun on the ground and pushing the dry leaves away with his feet so they wouldn't make any noise. Wolf appeared nearby and watched.

"Sit down," Brody said. "We are waiting to catch someone."

Wolf stared at them.

"He don't know what ye saying," Ames said.

Wolf walked into the woods and went out of sight.

"Where he going?"

"I don't know. He sure can make the hairs on the back of my neck come up."

Ames motioned with his head in the direction Wolf had gone. "Why he got dat pony-tail on top?"

"Joseph said he was stuck in his old ways. I guess that's how some of the Cherokee wear their hair, but don't make fun of him, Ames. Don't make him mad."

"Trust me, I ain't wanting him mad at me," Ames said. "He looks like a tough old goat."

As the sun sank low, Brody and Ames talked. Ames said he believed the thieves could be along anytime between dusk and daylight. The darker it got, the lower their voices became.

"Are you sure they are going to come through here?"

"Purt near. We gonna get 'em fer sure." Ames dug around in his pocket. "Got luck on our side."

"You got some kind of good luck charm there?" Brody thought he caught sight of a bright glint between Ames's fingers.

Ames quickly put it back in his pocket. "That's what I call it." Placing a finger across his lips, he shushed Brody. "Quit talking, now. We got some no-good thieves to catch."

Brody stayed quiet for a minute or two. "How you been feeling?" he whispered.

"My old knee been hurting, but it getting some better."

"I wasn't wondering about your leg."

Ames picked up a leaf, pinched the stem between his fingers, and spun it around. "Doing fine. Just hunky dorey."

The sun disappeared behind the horizon, and darkness took over. Frogs chirped, and an owl hooted in the distance. Something rustled in the brush, but it sounded too small to be a person. The gentle breeze held a slight chill.

Ames leaned over and kept his voice low. "Told you a lie. I ain't been doing so well."

"You still sleeping outside?" Brody said quietly.

"Most times them walls just close in on me."

"You spent too many years out there alone. It's just going to take some more time."

"I miss them smells," Ames whispered. "After a rain on the mountain it smell so good. And the quiet. Weren't no folks always chattering and carrying on. A man could keep his thoughts all together." He lowered his voice even more, and Brody strained to catch the words. "Them days weren't all bad."

"I remember," Brody said.

"I remember some of our days on Devil's Backbone but not all of 'em. I don't miss that hazy feeling, but I miss most everything else."

Brody chuckled quietly. "You did have some hazy days. You threatened to kill me, half a dozen times I think."

Ames stayed quiet for a while. "Glad them hazy days is gone."

Shifting against the tree, Brody found a more comfortable position. "My shoulder is a little sore."

"It are?"

"You nearly jerked my arm off when you dragged me out of the field."

Ames didn't say anything.

"It's not hurt bad. I know you were just keeping me out of trouble."

"I should'a not run. Guess old Ames is good at running off."

"You are not," Brody said, louder than he should have. "You are not," he repeated in a whisper.

"Remember them battles I told ye about."

"I remember. You told me you ran off like a coward, but I've seen you fight a bear and a killer madman. You did those things and saved my life, Ames. You are not a coward."

"It sure enough feel like it sometimes," Ames said.

Brody scoffed, "If it wasn't so dark, I'd poke you in the eye."

Ames snorted.

Brody continued. "I'd do it too, but it would just make you more ornery."

Ames pretended to be offended and snorted louder. Brody tried shushing him, but he was having a hard time not laughing out loud. After a few more chuckles, they finally quieted down.

Brody yawned. "Can you listen for them by yourself for a while?"

"Sure," Ames said.

"Wake me up in about an hour and we'll eat Mary's cornbread before I take watch."

Brody leaned back, crossed his arms over his chest, and let the crickets and frogs sing him to sleep.

He woke to screams.

Chapter Four

Early morning light had come and brought with it screaming, shouting, and squawking. Before he could get up, a boy ran past with a chicken flogging him. Brody rubbed his eyes.

"Get it off!" the kid howled.

A younger boy sprinted by with more chickens in hot pursuit. "Wait! Don't leave me! They're gonna kill me!"

"Aaaggghhh!" the first one shrieked.

Brody made it to his feet and ran around the tree in time to see Ames tackle the bigger boy. As they fell to the ground, eggs splattered everywhere. Just as fast as they went down, Ames popped back up with runny yolk on his face and a mad rooster spurring at the backs of his legs.

Twisting around, he grabbed at the chicken but missed. "Get this devil away from me!"

The smaller boy dodged around the trees, trying to lose the squawking and very agitated hens. While Ames spun in a circle, desperately trying to block the red rooster's lunges, he collided with the young boy. Both of them tripped and fell and were immediately flogged by the mad chickens.

The older boy got up, egg dripping off his shirt and pants. He eyeballed the situation the younger one was in, then turned on his heels . . . and ran headlong into Wolf. The sturdy man seemed to hardly move at all. When the youngster tried to pick himself up off the ground, Wolf glared at him. The boy slowly and carefully sat back down.

Ames swatted at the angry rooster. "Get!" he shouted. "Get on outta here!"

Brody could not help himself. He laughed so hard he doubled over, clutching his gut.

"Those chickens got the best of you?" he managed to say between laughs. Ames growled at him and kicked at the flapping rooster, but it nimbly dodged his foot. It saw an opportunity and grabbed the flesh on Ames's leg with its beak and twisted. Ames yelped and slapped at the bird while it deftly hopped out of reach.

The younger boy tried to run, but he fell and was immediately set upon by the hens, causing him to scream in fear and pain. All humor gone, Brody dashed to his aid and pinned one of the biddies down, gripping the wings close to the body.

The hen's frantic cries diverted all attention toward Brody, and the remaining chickens immediately headed for him. Hanging on to the screeching hen, he ran for the coop. When he reached the door, he yanked it open and flung her in. Other chickens in the coop squawked and scattered.

Brody remembered the cornbread in his pocket. He pulled it out and tossed it into the coop then hid behind the door. The mad hens made a beeline past him, clucking and calling, with the rooster right behind them. Brody slammed the door shut and leaned against it to catch his breath. The rooster crowed—in victory, it seemed to Brody.

When he came back, he witnessed a sight that nearly sent him into another bout of laughter. Ames had grabbed the older boy, who looked to be about twelve, by the ear with one hand and the younger boy's ear with his other. All of them were egg-spattered, and both kids were wailing.

"They gonna kill us, Clyde!" wailed the youngest. Brody guessed he was about nine.

Yellow egg yolk trailed down the side of Ames's face. "Ye done made me mad, tree-kicking mad."

Both boys were black and little more than skin and bones.

The smaller one was wearing only baggy cut-off britches. He was scratched up from his battle with the chickens. Brody could not help but feel a little sorry for them, considering the state they were in.

Ames let go of their ears. "What your names? And don't ye be lying to me, I'll have none of that."

The taller boy lowered his head. "Clyde."

The young boy wiped dirt and sweat from his face. "I'm his brother. I'm Albert."

"You boys have stolen a bunch of eggs," Brody said. "That's serious."

Wolf walked over and stood near Brody.

Albert's chin began to quiver. "They gonna kill us, Clyde. They gonna give us to that Indian and he gonna scalp us!" Tears welled up and spilled down his cheeks.

"I told you not to try and take a chicken," Clyde accused his brother.

Ames took the boys by their arms and started toward the house with them. Brody gathered up his rifle and Ames's musket. Wolf followed them toward the house, and for the first time, he seemed to find something interesting nearby instead of on the horizon.

They made a strange sight, Brody was sure, as Ames marched the boys up to the porch. The yellow dog ran up to the boys, wagging his tail, and began licking egg off of them. Ames scowled. "Fine watchdog, ain't ye? I ought to take ye out back and put a bullet in yer dadgum head."

The younger boy was still sniffling. "It ain't his fault. We give him an egg every time we come so he would like us and wouldn't bark none."

Ames muttered something under his breath, and the boy started to cry again. "Please, mister, please don't whip me!"

"Mary!" Ames shouted. "Mary, come on out here."

There was a rustling in the house, and the door started to open. "Did you catch the egg . . ." Mary started to ask, and then her voice trailed off as she caught sight of the children.

She looked from the boys to Ames, and the corners of her mouth slowly inched upward. Her sweet laughter rang out. "You sure did. You caught them."

"Why you tickled?" Ames asked, frowning.

Still grinning, she went inside, returned with a wet dishrag, and then tossed it to Ames. "Clean yourself up. You look like you're wearing a dozen eggs."

Ames wiped his face and arms. "Well, it ain't funny. These boys are in big trouble."

Albert covered his face, smearing even more dirt and yolk in the process. "We sorry. We real sorry."

Mary's expression softened. She took the wet rag from Ames and began to clean the muck off of Albert's face. "Where do you live, child?"

"Our house is through them woods over there," Clyde said.

"Why have you been stealing our eggs?"

"We had to," Albert said. "We ain't got much food, and Momma been sick."

"Our daddy died a few years back." Clyde motioned toward his brother. "We only took the eggs 'cause we was hungry."

Wolf sat on the edge of the porch and watched.

Luke came over the top of the hill. He was leading a mule. "What was all that commotion?"

"We caught the egg thieves," Brody said.

"What we gonna do with 'em?" Ames asked Mary.

"Go talk to their momma, I guess."

"We are real sorry," Clyde said. "We won't do it anymore."

"You are going to have to pay us back for all those eggs," Mary said.

Clyde vigorously nodded his head up and down. "Yes'um. Sure thing, we—"

Albert butted in. "But Clyde, we don't have no money."

Clyde reached over and thumped his brother. "Albert, you better shut your mouth."

Luke laughed and tied his mule up to the ring on the post.

Mary came over to Brody and motioned for Ames. "Let me talk to you two for a moment." They huddled close, and Mary lowered her voice. "We can't let this family go hungry."

"Can't let 'em keep on stealing," Ames said.

Brody looked at Ames thoughtfully. "You said you needed help."

Ames shook his head. "We can't afford—"

"No. Don't pay them money," Brody said. "Let them work for eggs."

"And vegetables," Mary added. "When the crops start to produce."

Ames looked pleased at that and placed a hand on Mary's shoulder. "You got breakfast started?"

"I do."

"Bacon?"

"Yes."

"Bring some out."

Mary went inside, and when she came out she was carrying a plate loaded with bacon and biscuits.

Albert's eyes grew wide and he licked his lips.

"Brody," Ames said. "You and . . ." He pointed at Wolf. "Y'all get in there and eat. I gonna take 'em home and be back in a few."

Eager hands reached for the food. Ames took a biscuit and broke it apart to place several bacon strips between the halves. Albert and Clyde followed suit, each making his own bacon sandwich.

"You boys don't cram all that in your mouth at once!" Mary chided.

Albert mumbled around a mouthful of biscuit, "You not gonna whip us?"

Ames shook his head. "Nope, but ye young'uns better be ready for some hard work. Now let's get ye on home."

"Yes, sir," they chimed in unison.

Everybody else headed to the house. Brody noticed Wolf's horse was saddled and standing patiently by the porch. It reminded him why he had come all the way out here.

"Mary, I'm going to saddle Buck up. I'll be back in just a minute."

Luke spoke up. "Don't you worry none 'bout that, Brody. I need to turn the other mule out to graze, and I can take care of your horse too."

"Thank you, Luke. That's mighty nice of you."

He followed Mary inside and set his and Ames's guns in the corner. When Wolf did not come in, Brody stuck his head back out. "You want something to eat?"

Wolf looked at him but remained on the porch.

Pretending to eat, Brody made chewing motions. "Food? You want some food?" When Wolf did not acknowledge him, he gave up and went to the table.

Mary placed a cathead biscuit, some bacon, and a couple of fried eggs in front of him. "Go ahead and eat. There's butter and jam. I've already had mine, and Anna left early to sell eggs down at the market."

She settled into a chair across from him. "Is Amos leaving with you?"

Brody met her eyes. He could see the worry in them. "The bounty hunters won't quit 'til they find us. I talked him into seeing Deputy Reeves in Fort Smith. Joseph told me he was a good man, and it would be the best thing to do."

He hung his head. "And there's something else. Joseph is ate up with worry over Todd. My folks took him with them. I promised Joseph after I came to warn Ames about the bounty hunters, I would come back and help him find his boy."

"Oh, Brody, what a mess. Do you know where they be?"

He nodded. "I think so, but you don't need to know, in case . . ."

Mary pinched her lips together tight. She nodded.

Luke came in and joined Brody at the table. He filled his plate up and bit into a biscuit.

"Do you think they will put him in jail?" Mary asked.

"Put who in jail?" Luke asked.

Glancing his way, she said, "Swallow your food and hush."

Brody pushed his plate away. He did not feel like eating anymore. "I just don't know. We both might go to jail. The law still wants us, but I'm trusting they will listen to the truth."

"I think it would kill him." Mary leaned over the table. "Amos still can't sleep in the house. Getting locked up would muddle him up even more. I don't believe he would last long at all."

Luke spoke around a mouthful of bacon, "She's right, Brody. Amos gets jumpy as a long-tail cat in a room full of rockers when he's inside four walls for very long."

"It's a risk we have to take," Brody said. "The Millers are gonna get us for sure. It's just a matter of time. Billy wants us dead—and he wants to be the one to do it."

"I hoped coming here would put all our troubles behind us. We bought this place and started working the land for us . . ." She hesitated. "For us! Not sharecropping, not working for no one but us, something to pass on to our children and our grandchildren. When we bought this place after escaping the Millers, I prayed to God that we would have peace."

Luke reached over and covered Mary's hand with his.

Brody felt a lump in his throat. The last thing he ever wanted was to bring sadness to this family. "I just know that if we don't do anything, they will find us sooner or later. In order to find us, they will hurt whoever is in their way."

Mary shook her head. "I'm scared plumb to death for both of you."

"We will be careful, I promise," Brody said. "If those bounty hunters show up, you need to tell them that we are in Indian Territory."

He turned to Luke. "No arguing with them. Make sure you tell them that you haven't seen Ames in weeks and that you figure he's hiding out there. They burned my folks' house down. Don't give them a reason to do it here."

Luke rocked back in his chair in shock, and Mary gasped. "What about your folks?"

"We made it out." Brody's voice was grim.

Wolf stepped in the doorway, speaking Cherokee.

Thundering footsteps rattled the floorboards on the porch. Wolf stepped aside, letting Clyde and Albert spill into the room.

Gasping for a good breath, Clyde bent over and put his hands on his knees. "They . . . they . . ."

"They chasing him!" Albert shouted.

Mary covered her mouth. "Lord have mercy."

Chapter Five

Brody grabbed his gun. Running past the boys, he jumped off the porch but then skidded to a stop. "Where? Where did it happen?"

Clyde came down the steps with Albert right behind him. "Just down the road there." He pointed.

"What happened?" Brody demanded.

"We was walking and seen some men come around a bend. They spotted us and kicked their horses up."

Albert pushed past his brother. "The man. What's his name, Clyde?"

"Ames," Clyde said with annoyance. "He turned us around and said to run back here."

Brody started for his horse again but paused. "How many men?"

"Three," Clyde said.

"Two," Albert said.

"There was three."

"No, there was two."

"Was one of them wearing a red shirt?" Brody asked.

"Yes," Clyde answered.

"They was all wearing brown," Albert said.

The two boys continued to argue while Brody ran to Buck. He climbed up in a flash and sent the horse running up the road. Hearing a thud of hooves approaching, he looked back to see Wolf low on his spotted horse's neck, coming after him.

Soon he came to the crossroad and pulled Buck to a hard stop, Wolf's horse sliding back on his haunches right behind him. In the middle of the intersection lay a half-eaten biscuit.

Jumping down, Brody inspected the ground for tracks. The road was mucked up with hoofprints, some overlaying what looked like Ames's boot prints. The boys' footprints were clear where they had turned and run.

"Brody!" Luke yelled as he rode up on a mule. "Where is he?"

"I don't know which way they went," Brody replied. "There are too many tracks."

"Was it the bounty hunters?"

Brody stared down the road that led to Fort Smith. "It had to be."

Wolf appeared beside him and knelt close to the ground. He used his finger to trace the outline of a boot track. Looking all around them, he pointed to a nearby stretch of trees and spouted off some words Brody didn't understand.

"What are we going to do?" Luke asked.

Brody got back in the saddle. "Miller's men will take him straight to Billy. We can catch them on the Fort Smith road."

"How we gonna get Amos away from 'em?"

"I'll figure out something." Brody started down the road. "Come on."

Wolf shouted and pointed at the ground.

Brody pulled Buck up short. "What is it?"

Gesturing toward the woods, Wolf walked a few steps and motioned for them to follow.

"We have to head toward town," Brody argued.

Wolf glowered at him, his face more angry than normal. He pointed to the ground, took two steps toward the woods, and pointed once more.

Brody got down and walked toward Wolf. "I think he's saying that Ames went this way."

Luke joined him, leading the mule and their horses. They followed the Indian as he led them into the big timber. At a low spot, the ground was damp. Ames had gone across the middle of it, sliding as he ran. Horse tracks dotted the ground on each side of the depression. Wolf circled the spot and found some scuffed-up leaves. He pointed to the left.

Brody had spent a year in Indian Territory tracking with Joseph. He knew that if you rushed, you would lose the trail—or worse, ruin it with your own prints. With Ames—his closest friend in the world—facing danger, Brody had to keep his wits about him, but it was very hard to do.

They trailed Ames and his pursuers for another few hundred steps until they reached a rocky area. Wolf examined stones in several directions but couldn't decide which way they had gone.

"Luke, tie up your mule and go down the draw that way." Brody said. "We'll go this way and see if we can pick up any sign."

Luke nodded and started working his way around the rocks and trees.

Wolf got on his horse. Brody mounted Buck and followed him up the hill. The Indian leaned over, nearly sideways on his mount while studying the ground. Brody wondered how he kept from falling.

They moved slowly, searching for any signs indicating that Ames or the horses had been through this part of the woods. After a few minutes Brody saw a broken pine sapling. "This way. This way!"

He reined Buck past the broken tree. Through the woods ahead, he saw a long straight tract. "It's the road. I knew we should have stayed on the road!"

Taking off in a gallop, he and Wolf moved swiftly down the trail. Buck stretched out his neck, and his powerful hooves struck the dirt hard, sending up clods of earth.

Brody's thoughts turned back to Ames. He felt like such an idiot for letting Wolf take time to track. They should have gone ahead and taken the south road right away. They would have a hard time catching them now. He was sure they were going to take Ames to Billy's house. Billy Miller was the low kind of man that had to torment his victim before exacting revenge. Brody might still have chance to save him, if he could get there in time.

Buck's rhythm was still strong when they hit the main road. Without hesitation, Brody turned his horse toward Fort Smith and kicked him into a full run.

Soon Buck started to blow hard, his neck lathered with foamy sweat. Brody pulled him back to a trot to cool down. He should not have let his irritation with Wolf make him run his horse full out. That—and fear for Ames—was causing him to make poor choices.

Wolf's horse pounded up beside him, and the Indian reined the spotted horse back to match Buck's trotting pace. He was still scowling, which prompted Brody to frown back at him. After a length of pondering on it, he felt his dander rising. "You need to go find Joseph."

Wolf ignored him.

"Hey! I don't need your help. You don't even know who is a good guy and who is a bad guy. Oh, that's right, we are all bad guys." Brody was shouting by now, and that got Wolf's attention. The Indian hissed under his breath and kicked his horse up into a gallop.

Brody kicked Buck's sides and raced after him. He had to find Ames. Keeping the horses to a ground-eating lope, they overtook a wagon on the road. The driver stared as they dashed past.

The horses' hooves thumped against the dirt road in a constant rhythm, but when both horses began to labor heavily, Brody slowed Buck to a trot again. Wolf followed suit.

After a few minutes of cooldown, Brody caught a glimpse of two riders disappearing into a curve far down the road. His pulse leapt into a new rhythm.

One of the men was clearly wearing a red shirt.

Yanking back on the reins, Brody brought Buck to a halt and threw out a hand to stop Wolf.

We shouldn't be on the road.

Chapter Six

Ames had taught him to stay in the woods when traveling, hidden from view, but here he was out in the wide open. Wolf watched and waited for Brody.

Buck snorted loudly and shook his head, causing the metal on his bridle to rattle and clink. Brody turned in the saddle to look for a good place to get off the track.

Wolf grunted. Brody looked over to see him pointing down the road. The two figures had doubled back and were coming fast.

Brody jerked back on the reins and kicked Buck so hard he reared up. It only lasted a second, but to Brody the horse seemed to stall for an eternity. As soon as Buck's hooves touched down, he plunged into the woods. The sudden momentum sent Brody to the very back edge of the saddle. He struggled to regain his seat, and looking over his shoulder, he saw Wolf's horse dashing back the way they had come.

Hoofbeats drummed the road as the riders closed the distance. A quick glance confirmed his fear. It was the bounty hunters.

Brody needed distance between him and his pursuers. He needed speed.

Trusting his horse, he let Buck choose the way. The horse sprinted though the big woods, changing course only when a tree or the terrain blocked their path. Brody resisted the urge to turn him. He wanted to be sneaky, to double back or cut around toward the road. Instead, he kept nudging the horse's flanks.

They came to a wide crooked creek running around the base of a ridge. Tightening his grip on the reins, Brody started to pull back but stopped.

Distance. Speed. Trust the horse.

Just as they reached the edge, he regretted his decision. The creek bank dropped down at least three feet, and on the other side of the wide stream the bank rose higher by another foot.

Buck hardly slowed. He shot between some saplings and jumped for the other side. Brody grabbed the saddle horn and held on with all his strength.

Buck's intentions and courage were admirable, but the horse came up a few feet short and they crashed against the opposite side. Buck's belly smashed against the lip of the bank. The horse wheezed as the air was knocked out of him. The jolting stop sent Brody flailing over Buck's head. A low-hanging limb twisted Brody around in mid-air, and he landed hard on the ground.

Pawing at the bank, Buck struggled to get up the incline. Brody rolled away to avoid the horse's hooves. As soon as Buck made it up, he drew a massive breath. His sides heaved over and over as his lungs struggled to catch up.

"Easy, boy," Brody whispered. He got to his feet and looked back across the creek. He couldn't see the bounty hunters, but he could hear them shouting as their horses' hooves snapped dead limbs. Climbing onto Buck, he turned him and headed up the ridge. He kept the horse at barely more than a walk, but Buck felt different under him, soft and wobbly. He rubbed his horse's neck. "It's okay, Buck, you'll be okay."

At the top of the hill, they didn't pause. Following the ridge line, Brody kept going until he found a suitable route down. He pulled the reins against Buck's neck and turned him down the incline. Buck stumbled.

Brody leaned back in the saddle, and the horse slid for a few seconds before regaining his footing. They continued down, sliding often, until they reached the bottom of the hill. Brody jumped off the saddle and listened. He could hardly hear anything over his horse's labored breathing.

After a few moments, Brody led Buck north through the

woods. They had to keep moving. Their mad dash over the ridge had surely left a trail a blind man could follow.

He walked until his legs burned. His feet hurt, and his butt was bruised from falling off the horse, but that didn't bother him near as much as something that kept eating at him.

He hadn't seen Ames with those two men. On top of that, Wolf had gone a different direction. Brody hadn't seen him since then. He worried what would happen if the bounty hunters had caught Joseph's father.

Stopping at a tiny brook, Brody drank, then ran his hands down the buckskin's legs while Buck slurped at the water. Brody was grateful that his horse seemed fully recovered from his fall earlier. His breathing was better, and there was no swelling or fever in any of his joints.

A squirrel's claws scratched against a pine tree as it ran up, and a hawk let out a shrill call in the distance. The forest was alive, but the bounty hunters were not within earshot. Brody's tired bones told him to stop for a while, but he knew that was not an option. He had to keep going. He just had to decide which way.

After leading Buck for another half-hour, Brody stopped and draped the reins across the horse's neck. Buck's hide had dried, leaving his hair feeling crusty from the sweaty lather. Brody twisted some dried grass together and rubbed him down while the horse nibbled at the weeds.

When he finished, Brody looked around at the thick woods. As the minutes passed, he hardly moved. Fear kept him from picking a direction to travel.

He rubbed Buck's neck. "I don't know which way to go." The horse stopped chewing for a moment as if he was also pondering their situation. Brody wondered how far they had gone. Their frantic pace had carried them miles in the wrong direction, away from Ames.

"We need to double back." He closed his eyes and leaned his

head on Buck's neck. "Lord, please let Ames and Wolf be okay. I'm pretty lost about everything right now."

Buck reached around and lipped at his shirtsleeve. Brody sighed and opened his eyes.

"You're a pretty tough horse, you know that?" he said affectionately.

A sudden rattling made Brody jump. He searched for the direction the sound was coming from, and through the woods to his left he caught a glimpse of two horses in traces.

He scrambled up on Buck and walked him to a better vantage point. A dim road curled around, following a twisting creek. A man, his wife, and young child were in the wagon attached to the horses, and they were heading north.

"Howdy," Brody called their way.

The man stopped his horses and watched as Brody rode towards them. They were a young couple, and looked to be in their late twenties. Between them sat a little girl who was maybe six or seven. The man's hair was red as fire, and his skin was white as a deer's belly.

"Howdy," Brody repeated.

The woman pulled the little girl close and looked to her husband. The man glanced at her and then looked Brody over, seeming none too impressed with his disheveled appearance. "What do you want?"

"I need to get to Fort Smith," Brody said.

The man pointed back the way they had come. "Go that way, south."

"Thanks," Brody said. "I got separated from a friend of mine while we were hunting. Have you seen anybody else on this road?"

"Not a soul."

The little girl squirmed in her seat. "But what about . . ."

The mother squeezed the child's arm, shaking her head.

Pulling on his horse's reins, the redheaded man backed the wagon off the road. He motioned toward Brody. "Come on. We can ride with you for a ways." He guided the horses into a tight turn until they were back on the road facing the direction they had just came from.

Brody's brow wrinkled with confusion. "I don't need any company."

"Sure you do," the man said. "There is a junction back there. We should make sure you go the right way."

Suspicion crept over Brody.

The girl looked up at her father. "Those men are . . ." The mother clamped a hand over the girl's mouth and looked at Brody with fear in her eyes.

It was clear what was waiting for him on the road. The bounty hunters were still looking for him, telling everyone they saw to be on the lookout for someone about fifteen with a large scar through his eyebrow.

No telling what else they were saying. Horse thief. Murderer.

Without another word, Brody whirled Buck and headed north. He looked over his shoulder in time to see the man whipping up his horses. The young couple would tell of their encounter, and the bounty hunters would be back on his trail any moment.

He kicked Buck's sides and raced up the road. They stayed on the road for a mile or so and then cut off into the woods. A ridge line took them north and then curled east.

The long ridge seemed to go on forever. Rocks and cliffs jutted out of its sides. No matter which path he picked, there were dips, boulders, and old downed trees. It was the roughest country he had ever seen.

Their progress slowed to a careful walk, and when the ridge bottomed out, Brody paused to look for another rise he could climb in order to double back. Somewhere behind him a rock bounced and whacked against a tree as it rolled down the side. Listening intently, he waited until another stone clacked down the hill. "They are still dogging us, Buck," he whispered.

Continuing into the thick wilderness, Buck squeezed

between two boulders. Brody had to pull his feet up to keep from getting them caught. When he found the bend of a creek, he followed its edge for a while. Above them were massive rocks and ridges of stone.

A heavily used game trail caught his eye, and he took it. It led up a hillside, away from the creek. The grade was such that Brody had to get down and lead Buck. His hooves slipped on the rocks, causing the horse to nearly fall. Brody stopped and backed him behind a tall, smooth boulder. Once he felt Buck was well hidden, he grabbed his rifle hanging from the saddle.

The stock he had carved felt good in his hands. Most of the whittled ridges had been worn smooth, and each gouge was a testament to the rifle's long journey.

Ames had given the broken gun to him, and Brody had mended it into something special. He had already proved it was deadly in his hands, though he had no desire to put a bullet in a person. He really hoped it would not come to that. He was already in a big mess. Being blamed for another death wouldn't make it any better. Resting on a rock, he watched the creek bottom and waited.

An hour passed as shadows fell across the ridge. Every now and then, he would hear Buck shift his weight or heave a sigh.

A chipmunk scurried around the boulder and froze when it saw Brody. Its nose wiggled, and then the animal skittered into a rock crevice and out of sight. After a moment it ran out the other side and around behind him.

Brody watched as the comical creature bounced from one rock to another. Leaning to the side, he noticed the chipmunk had gone up a dim trail. Upon inspection, he found the path had not been traveled in a long while. While it was faint, it was clearly a trail up the side.

The steep rocky path was no place for Buck. The tired horse was still ground tied where he had left him, dozing with one back foot slack. He pricked his ears as Brody came closer. "Sorry, boy, but I have to leave you behind a little while. Stay put and rest up." He rubbed his head, then turned back to the trail.

Using trees to keep from sliding back, Brody made his way up. The rocks were bigger near the top, with a massive wall of stone on his right.

The sound of splashing water and chirping frogs caught his attention. It was coming from higher on the hillside. He kept going until he found a tiny waterfall spilling over a little ledge and falling ten feet down on moss-covered rocks.

Brody had never seen anything so beautiful, and for the briefest of moments he felt like a kid again. The urge to slip his boots off and dip his sore feet in the cool water was almost irresistible.

Above the sound of frogs and splashing water Brody thought he heard a voice. He held his breath and tried to hear anything out of the ordinary. After a moment, he began to think he had imagined it.

"He's here," a voice called out.

The hairs on Brody's neck stood tall. He gripped his rifle tight.

They couldn't have tracked me this far!

Someone shouted, "I found his horse!"

Brody scrambled past the waterfall and up some loose rocks to finally reach a level spot. On his right was a stone wall with a diagonal crack in the face of the rock. The opening was wide at the bottom and narrow at the top, and it looked fairly deep.

He worked his way into the crack. When he felt he was concealed deep enough by the shadows, he stopped. His heart was hammering.

I'm an idiot. I'm an idiot.

He wanted to kick his own rear for dropping his guard. He strained to hear the sounds of pursuit, but there were no voices or unusual sounds. Finally, he relaxed a bit against the stone. The angle made it almost comfortable.

His mind churned with possible plans. Darkness would come within an hour, but he would have to wait until the middle of the night to sneak out of his hiding place. After finding the bounty hunters' camp, the last trick would be to get Buck without the men knowing.

A pebble tumbled from above and bounced across the ground near Brody's hiding spot.

"Come around to this side," a man hollered. "There's a path down there." Brody's heart thumped harder. He kept still and breathed in quick shallow breaths.

Someone walked along the crest of the ridge just above him. A scattering of stones clattering down the path below alerted him to the other bounty hunter working his way up towards him. Brody was going to be caught.

He twisted around and peered farther into the crack. It angled upward and seemed to get smaller, but at the very top he saw a small amount of light. The tiny passage went all the way up, but he couldn't be certain the opening was big enough for him to squeeze through.

A shower of rocks rolled down, accompanied by a grunt as one of the men struggled for footing. He had very little time left before discovery.

He felt like nothing more than a trapped rabbit. He had stalked them before and witnessed the moment they realized danger was near. They would freeze in place until the last possible moment and then explode out of their hiding spot in a mad dash for safety. Brody was at that very point and out of options. He took a deep breath and sprinted out of the angled crevice. He turned right, glancing over his shoulder.

The bounty hunter with the red shirt let out a yell and fell back on the steep slope. He grabbed a tree root to stop his slide and locked eyes with Brody. The man shouted to his companion on top of the rise. "There he goes! Get down here!"

A shot rang out, and a bullet whizzed off a nearby rock.

Without looking back, Brody dove toward an opening in the ground. He crawled across the dusty earth and fell into the mouth of a cavern.

After dropping a couple of feet, he crashed onto a large flat rock. He lost his grip on the Henry rifle and it slid off the rock and disappeared over the edge. Scrambling to his feet, he looked to see his gun lying on the cave floor four feet below. He jumped down just as a voice echoed inside the cavern.

"He's down there!"

Brody grabbed his rifle and ran into the darkness. The cool, moist air chilled his sweaty skin. He rounded a sharp bend in the cave, and within a few steps he reached complete blackness. After another six or seven steps, he stopped.

He was being unwise. Panic had erased his wits. There could be another drop-off that would send him tumbling down. A broken leg would get him caught for sure. Running into a jagged wall wouldn't feel good either. He waited and listened.

The men jumped down to the flat rock, their boots slapping against the hard surface. After a moment, the thuds and crunch of pebbles meant they had taken the last leap down into the cave.

"Where are you, boy?" one of the men asked. His voice was gruff.

"He's in here, Carl. Somewhere," the other man said in a nasally whine. "Come on out! We know you're in here."

The urge to run came over him again, but Brody clamped down on it. If he could not see them, then they could not see him. He would simply hide in the dark until they gave up.

The men waited for a few seconds. "Lester, go back down the hill and get a lantern," the man with the deeper voice ordered. "I'll wait here."

They would find him. His run was about to be over. He couldn't let them take him to the Millers. He had to figure a way out and then get to Ames. He could not give up. Not without a fight.

He waited until he heard one of the bounty hunters trying to climb out of the cavern. Brody let the noise cover the sound of his footsteps as he eased forward, hand outstretched. His fingers scraped on the rough edges of a rock wall. Using it to guide him, he moved deeper into the darkness.

"Push me up," the one with the high-pitched voice said.

"I am pushing, Lester, dangit."

Brody noticed that the soft noises coming from his boots on the cave floor seemed to change, and the air felt a little different. He reached out until his knuckles touched rock. The cave had pinched in and became narrower as he went. After a few more steps, he reached a dead end. All had grown quiet with the bounty hunters. Brody put his back to the wall and waited. It was all he could do.

Long minutes passed. He ran his hand over the Henry rifle for reassurance. There were about a dozen cartridges in the gun. He could hold them off for a while, until the bullets ran out. The rest were in the saddlebag on Buck's back.

He thought of trying to run by them, maybe shooting and dashing past while they took cover. One of the men would surely hit him at such close range, though. He would make a nice target while trying to climb up the flat rock and out of the cave.

"Here," Lester's voice echoed. "Take this."

There was the sound of the man jumping back down. "Light it up," Carl said. "Here we come, boy."

The pitch black began to brighten. A host of shadows started to take shape and jump crazily, forming jagged demon claws coming closer and closer.

The bounty hunters' feet shuffled, and the light grew. "You better come on out."

Brody's hopes of finding a hiding spot were crushed. Panic squeezed the breath out of him. He could see the walls in the growing light. Looking around, he saw no other way out, nothing but rock.

Chapter Seven

A gentle wave of air moved over the top of his head, then fanned his face. Brody craned his head back and saw the faintest outline of an opening a ways up. Amongst the panic, he felt a stirring of hope.

He strained to reach the edge with his fingertips, but they were just short of it. There was no way around it. He was going to have to make a lot of noise.

He hurriedly tossed his gun up and over the edge. Leaping, he grabbed the lip of rock and pulled as hard as he could. Fear pushed him up, and he scrambled onto the ledge. He saw a passage, but the ceiling was so low he had to crawl.

He heard a shout behind him, echoing up through the tunnel. Rushing on blindly, he felt his way along the hard corridor. The farther he went, the stronger the breeze grew, as did a pale light. When he reached a small opening, Brody squeezed through and across some sharp rocks. He tumbled out into the dusky evening.

Hastening to his feet, he ran across a flat section below the crest of the ridge, weaving between broken boulders and rocks while looking for another hiding spot. His legs and lungs burned, but he still ran, doing his best not to get his foot caught in the cracks of the rocks or to sink into a leaf-covered hole.

One big boulder sat at the base of some massive stones jutting up from the mountainside. Brody ducked behind it and found another dark opening in the space between the stones. The hidden entrance was smaller than that of the first cave he had found but high enough that it allowed him to stand straight.

He had to make a quick decision. He could try to run for it and take the slim chance the two bounty hunters would miss him, or he could den up again. This smaller cave seemed to be a good spot, easy to overlook. The sun had disappeared behind the ridge. Night had already settled into the valley below. This cave would have to work until the bounty hunters went back to their camp.

Brody eased into the opening. Old leaves and twigs were matted down at the entrance, and something small skittered in the debris. Further inside he saw rocks and pebbles that had fallen from the ceiling; among them he spotted a few small white bones arranged in a strange pattern near the wall. Past the bones, the cave disappeared into darkness.

He checked his gun sights, just in case there was something hiding in the black shadows. Nerves on edge, he slowly moved forward into the dark, straining to listen for sounds in front of him, and behind.

The darkness swallowed him several paces further. Unwilling to go another step, Brody turned around. He could just make out the entrance to the cave, the dim light receding rapidly. He wished heartily for a wall against his back, but he did not know how far the cave went—or what might be hiding in there. The best he could do was feel his way to the side wall and sit down, legs crossed, with his gun across his lap.

Staring at the cave mouth, his mind raced. What would happen if the bounty hunters did not give up for the night? What if they kept looking and found him? His imagination would not turn off. Over and over he thought of the outcome.

A soft glow would come. The glow would become harsh, sending the shadows dancing as the bobbing lantern came closer. The men would be hidden from view behind the blinding light, but they would see him. Brody wondered if he could shoot the lantern. Even if it stopped them, he would still be trapped in this den.

He hit his thigh with his fist in frustration. The decision to hide here had been foolish after all. He should have just made a run for it. Maybe he still had time. Brody could still see the cave opening. It was now just a little lighter than the blackness around it. He got up and slipped toward the opening. When a mumbling of voices reached his ears he froze, but they remained the same, neither growing nor diminishing in volume.

Moving at a snail's pace, Brody eased up to the boulder that partially blocked the cave opening. He peeked around it and saw the men. The sight set his heart to hammering, blasting away in his chest as if dynamite was exploding over and over.

They were there! The men were setting up a cold camp just a few steps on the other side of the boulder. They put their bedrolls down and sat on them. Brody ducked behind the rock and listened.

"That boy is long gone," Lester said.

"Quiet," Carl commanded in a harsh whisper. "He is here. He's just hid somewhere."

"Can we eat now?"

"No. They ain't gonna be no eating. You sit right here and listen."

"Where you going?"

"I'm going to sleep. We'll take turns on watch."

"You sure that boy is still here somewhere?"

"He's here, and they ain't nobody who can walk on this rocky slope without making noise. Just stay quiet and listen."

Brody heard some shuffling, the sound of a bedroll being spread out, and then the men were silent. Brody rubbed his face in frustration. It was full dark now, and the bounty hunter was right. It would be nigh impossible to go anywhere without making noise.

Looking into the sky, he saw no moon, no light, and no hope of sneaking past the men. The only choice was to wait. Brody snuck back into the cave, placing his weight on each foot carefully to avoid crunching sounds. In the darkness his gun barrel scraped against the rock wall. He stopped instantly.

"Carl," Lester whispered loudly.

Brody had an overwhelming urge to run, but he fought it back.

"Hey, Carl . . . are you asleep?"

Brody heard a grunt, and then, "Whu—What? What did ya say? Did you hear something?"

"Yeah, I heard something. My stomach. My stomach is growling something awful. I sure am hungry."

"Lester, I'm gonna kill you dead if you don't shut your mouth and forget about food."

"I could eat a leather boot, right now," Lester grumbled.

"You can eat my boot when I shove it down your throat. Now shut up, and you better not wake me unless you hear that stupid kid trying to get away!"

"Wull, he must not be too stupid, or we'd a-done caught him by now. All right, all right, don't point your dang gun at me! I'll shut up." Lester mumbled for another few minutes and then got quiet.

Letting out a relieved breath, Brody slowly sat. He would check on the men in a while, hoping both of them would be sound asleep.

Lester's hunger had reminded him of his own. He wished for some of Momma's cooking, some chocolate gravy or fried chicken, anything.

Brody breathed in deep, then let it out. He was so tired of running and being chased. Heartbroken with worry, he wondered where Ames was. They probably had him tied up down at the bottom of the ridge with the horses. What if he was hurt . . . or worse? The situation made Brody feel so helpless.

He wondered if Joseph had found Todd yet. After his family had fled Fort Smith with little Todd in tow, they could have changed their minds about traveling to the old farm. What if Todd had fallen ill again? The closest doctor was in Fort Smith.

Thoughts of Doc Slaughter brought Sarah to mind, of course.

Doc's daughter had the most beautiful black curls and sparkling eyes. His pleasure in thinking about her did not last long, when he remembered her father had forbidden them to ever see each other again. He could hear the words Doc Slaughter spoke the night the Millers almost caught him, the night they burned his parents' house: *Sarah is in danger when she's around you.* His last memory of Sarah was the sight of her pretty face looking at him from a wagon as it disappeared into the dark—then she was gone.

Momma and Papa were gone with Todd, and now he had lost Buck. Joseph was out looking for his son. Ames was gone, he didn't know where. That thought sent Brody down another spiral. He had even managed to lose Wolf. Everyone Brody loved was scattered, and none of them knew where he was. He was so lost, he didn't even know where he was.

A low, mournful, howling cry filled the night, growing in volume and then fading away. Wolves! Brody clutched his gun closer. Papa had told him stories of wolves, of being stalked when he was hunting by himself. The pack had surrounded him and howled over and over, making him fear for his life. He had recounted how a warning shot from his gun had finally scattered them.

The bounty hunters were talking again, but Brody couldn't make out their mumbling from where he was. After a few seconds, they became quiet, surely listening for another howl.

Leaning back against the cave wall, Brody waited, but the wolf was silent. Just once it had howled. He wondered why, and what was it doing out there? It made him afraid in a different way than the bounty hunters did. He was grateful for the cave.

The longer he waited, the more his eyelids seemed to weigh. The events of the day had drained him. Running up steep hills had taken all the energy from his legs. His back ached, his butt was bruised, and his mind was exhausted.

Something touched his leg, jolting him awake. The early morning light kept his eyes from focusing for a moment. He rubbed them, and a brown-headed boy came into focus, sitting in front of Brody. The boy looked to be maybe thirteen, a couple of years younger than he was. He was clean and had a short haircut, but his clothes were those of a farmer, and about two sizes too big. Brody scooted away from the boy, kicking up dust as he went.

"Who—who are you?"

"Your friends already left," the boy replied.

Confused by the remark, Brody pondered for a moment.

"Are you okay?" the boy asked.

It all came back in a rush. Brody lunged up and ran to the huge boulder at the entrance to the cave. He peered cautiously around it and saw that the area just beyond was clear of men and bedrolls.

The boy came and stood next to him. "They are just down that slope a little ways. See yonder? What are y'all looking for?"

Brody spotted one of the men, moving downward slowly in a long arc. He was checking behind every rock and in each crevice. Ducking out of sight, Brody pulled the boy back, too. "They are not my friends."

"But they are searching for something, right?" The boy hiked his pants up higher.

There was an awkward silence while Brody tried to decide what to tell him. "Did they see you?"

Untying a rope from around his waist, the boy redid the knot, cinching it tighter. "They are looking for you, aren't they?"

Brody nodded. "Did they see you?" he repeated.

"No." The boy looked over the boulder. "Bad men?"

"Pretty bad."

Offering his hand, the boy said, "My name's Ray, Ray Donald, named after my uncle."

"My name's Brody, Brody Martin, named after . . . nobody, I guess." He shook hands with the boy. "Those men got my horse. It's a buckskin. Was it there?"

"Yes, a nice-looking buckskin and two ugly bays. That's how

I knew y'all were here. I seen them horses on a picket line down near the bottom. That's why I thought you were with them, there being three horses and all."

Brody spoke quickly. "Did you see a black man down there? He would have been tied up."

Ray dashed Brody's hopes. "Nope. No black man, tied up or otherwise."

"Oh."

"But I didn't go all the way down. There could have been a camp under the trees at the bottom. The leaves are pretty thick, and I could not see past the tops. He could have been there."

Brody hoped Ray was right. Maye he still had a chance to free Ames. He had to be down at the bottom of the ridge. There was no way the bounty hunters could have gotten Ames to Billy Miller and then back on his trail so quickly.

Dread filled him as he thought of another possibility. What if they had shot him dead and hid his body for safekeeping? They would do that . . . because they had *two* bounties to get.

"Your face sort of turned white just now." Ray was looking at him. "You okay? What else you want to know?"

Brody tried to push the thought away. He had to focus on his predicament right now. "I want to know where I am. Do you live here?"

"We have a farm not far from here. This is Lee Creek Valley, and you found my secret cave. I've been playing around here for years. You picked a good hiding spot because it's hard to see until you are right up on it."

Ray walked over and picked up a couple of the white bones. He polished them on his shirt sleeve, and then used one of them to point into the cave. "This one is deep. It goes back a long ways. The Indians called it the Devil's Den, though I ain't never found Old Scratch hiding in there."

Brody vaguely heard what Ray was saying. His attention was focused on finding a way out. "Can I get to the horses without—"

"Without those men getting you?"

Brody nodded.

"Who are they?" the boy asked.

"Bounty hunters."

Ray took a step back. "What have you gone and done?"

"I made someone mad." He sighed. "Someone with money."

Ray cocked his head. "Who are you again?"

"Brody Martin."

"Never heard of you."

"Billy Miller put a bounty on me for something I didn't do."

The boy shrugged and looked down. "Never heard of him, either. Say, that is a strange looking gun you got there."

"I carved the stock. The old one was broken."

Ray stared at him for a moment. He glanced from the gun to Brody's face, his clothes, his boots, and back to the gun. "You can't do it."

"I can't do what?"

"You can't get to the horses. Those men will be with the horses by now."

"I've got to get out of here. I can't waste any more time," Brody said. "A good friend of mine is in some big trouble."

"Like the trouble you are in?"

Brody hesitated. "Worse."

"I'll go get my father," Ray said matter-of-factly.

"No. You should get out of here." He looked at Ray's brown hair and eyes. "You look too much like me. Those men will shoot if they see you."

Ray pointed to his forehead. "What about your scar? That is different, and I am younger than you."

Shaking his head, Brody said, "These are the kind of men who will shoot first and look for a scar later."

Ray was silent for a moment. "Maybe I could help."

"Please just go and don't come back until I'm gone."

"You could come to my home."

"No. I don't want to get your family involved. The Millers are really bad. People get hurt when they try to help me."

Ray paused. "How are you going to get your horse back?"

"I'll be all right," Brody desperately insisted.

Ray turned to leave. "It was nice meeting you, Brody."

"Nice meeting you, too, but don't let them see you."

Ray leaned out to peer down the mountain. He looked back, waved once, and then disappeared around the boulder.

Chapter Eight

It would have been so easy to accept help, and just as easy for things to go wrong. Brody didn't want to bring trouble into any more lives. This mess was his to deal with.

He crept away from the cave quietly, stepping carefully so as not to disturb any pebbles or break any dead limbs. He stopped and stared down at the rocky steepness.

The men could be hiding in any of a thousand places. Massive stones, trees, and crevices provided the ultimate cover. Ames and Buck were somewhere at the bottom, and Brody needed to get down there badly.

He looked around, hoping a solution would come to him. A tall rocky outcropping on the right caught his attention. The shape of the stone formed the silhouette of a man's face, the sort of face Brody thought the devil himself might have. Goose flesh came up on his arms.

He couldn't see the men, but he figured they had set a trap on the path leading down. The only safe way would be to go higher on the ridge, and far enough out, before circling back and going down below to get Buck.

He climbed carefully. Some of the rocks were loose and rolled slightly under his feet. He planned each step, making sure no stones were sent tumbling and clacking down the incline. He found a faint trail that led straight along the ridge. He followed it while looking for a way to cut back down the mountain.

When he felt he had gone far enough along the ridge, Brody gingerly began to angle down toward the creek. It took a good while, and several times he nearly lost his footing before reaching the bottom.

The slope stopped just short of the creek, leaving a stretch of flat ground no more than twenty steps wide. Tall oaks towered over him and cast irregular shadows all around.

Buck would probably be tied within sight of the stream, but Brody wasn't sure how to stay hidden. From the high ground, the men could easily spot him slipping from tree to tree. While he was trying to decide what to do, a dead limb floated by and gave him an idea.

Quickly covering the distance to the creek bank, Brody entered the cool water, careful not to splash. It came up just past his waist, and he sucked in a quick breath as the cold temperature of the water shocked him.

He rested the rifle across his shoulder and hung onto roots that were exposed in the bank. Slowly he inched his way up the stream. The height of the bank was nearly perfect, hiding all of him except his head. As he moved, he watched the hillside like a hawk.

After thirty minutes of moving at a snail's pace, Brody disturbed a squirrel that scampered up a pine tree. Its claws dug in and sent debris falling down. The squirrel barked over and over, warning the other squirrels in the area, causing a few more tree rats to join in the melee.

Brody froze in place and waited. When he was hunting, the sound of a squirrel barking in the distance was a sure sign something was moving around in the woods. In his mind, he could see the bounty hunters jumping from their hiding spots, charging down the hill shouting and shooting. What would he do? Duck under the water and hold his breath?

A large cane patch across the creek looked appealing. The tall, segmented poles were crowded together and formed a thick wall of green that blocked the sun, creating a dark place to hide.

Brody waded across, then stepped on the bank and into the thicket. His feet felt like they weighed a ton from all the water in his boots. After squeezing deeper into the canes, he propped on a thick pole and tried to keep his balance as he took off one boot and poured the creek water out. He followed quickly with the other boot. The squirrels continued to bark.

About ten minutes passed before the tree rats' noise lessened to a whistling sound repeated over and over. He had never been sure why squirrels did this, but he suspected it was a way to announce the threat was gone. This time, the noise settled his nerves a bit. If the men were sneaking down the hill, the squirrels would definitely see them. They would be barking instead of whistling.

He weaved his way through the cane, staying just far enough in to conceal his movement. Using the gun barrel, he pushed young cane aside, careful to avoid stepping on the dead poles that littered the ground. They were dry and brittle and would snap louder that someone clapping their hands.

His family had cut cane when they cleared the farmland near Greenwood. His job was to throw it on the fire. The first time the cane started popping, he thought someone had tossed bullets into the flames. Each segment in the poles was a sealed chamber, and the heat from the fire would make the pressure inside rise. When the cane ruptured, it sounded very much like gunfire. He had never heard such a ruckus before.

The cane patch finally gave way to oaks and elms. Brody paused and watched the hillside. Some of the massive rocks looked familiar, but he couldn't be certain it was the same place where he had left Buck. The horses were nowhere to be seen, and neither were the bounty hunters or Ames. The men had moved somewhere else. They could be anywhere in the valley, and Brody wasn't sure how he was going to find them.

A twig snapped behind him. Seconds later, the brush rustled and he heard the sound of thumping footsteps. Brody bolted from the woods and rushed to the creek.

Someone cried out in pain. Looking back, Brody saw the bounty hunters. The one wearing the red shirt had Ray by the arm. The man twisted the boy's arm, causing him to shout out again.

"Get over here," the man said to Brody. He twisted Ray's arm again. Ray gritted his teeth and hissed in pain.

"Do it 'til he cries," the other man hollered gleefully. Brody recognized the nasally twang belonging to Lester.

"Stop it!" Brody yelled.

Lester gave him an evil grin. "Get over here, or Carl will break his arm clean off."

"I'm sorry," Ray whimpered. "Just let me go."

Lester had his pistol pointed at Brody. "You made a mistake sending him to steal our new buckskin."

"I didn't send him, and it's not your horse."

"That horse is ours now." Carl shoved Ray at Lester, who wrapped his gun hand across the boy's chest.

Brody brought his rifle to his shoulder in one smooth movement.

"Put it down!" Carl shouted, drawing his gun.

Carl thumbed the hammer back on his pistol, but Brody was already aiming. Releasing a breath, Brody pulled the trigger. There was a loud shot, and sparks flew from Carl's pistol as it was ripped from his hand.

Jacking another round into his rifle, Brody fired again and sent the bounty hunter's hat tumbling from his head. Fear spread across Carl's face as he stepped backward, stumbling and falling.

Lester swung his pistol back toward Brody, but Ray bit him on the hand. The bounty hunter hollered in pain and let the boy go.

Ray sprinted to Brody, and they ran into the creek. As Brody's feet hit the water he stumbled and flailed into the steam, one arm outstretched and the other holding the gun out of the creek. His legs churned under him as he pushed across. Just as he grabbed a root and started pulling himself up the bank, Lester fired his first shot.

"I'm gonna put a bullet in them quick feet!"

Brody rolled over the top of the bank into a crouch, jacking a shell in his gun. "Not yet," he spat. He fired. Brody's shot was purposely about two feet over Lester's head, but it did send the man scrambling behind a large rock, with Carl right behind him.

Ray stayed on Brody's heels as they ran around a boulder and up the hill.

A bullet whizzed through the air and splintered a nearby sapling, but they kept going. Their younger legs were putting distance between themselves and the bounty hunters. The pace grew excruciating, causing Brody's muscles to burn and his chest to heave. Another shot rang out.

"Let's get to the cave," Ray panted as they pushed up the mountain.

Brody's breaths were ragged, but he didn't slow down. Glancing back at Ray, he said, "No, we'll just be trapped again. We have to make it over the top and lose them in the woods."

"Brody, that cave is too deep for them to find us. It will work."

Brody had no choice. He had everything to lose if the bounty hunters caught them.

High on the ridge, he spotted the boulder hiding the entrance to the cave. Brody cut straight up the incline. "Follow me."

Ray was hard on Brody's heels. "They're coming."

Brody risked a look over his shoulder. The bounty hunters were much closer than he had expected. Lester stopped and fired in his direction. Brody leaped for cover but fell over a pile of rocks. The Henry rifle flew from his hands, slid across the ground, and fell into a crack next to the cliff wall. Getting to his feet, Brody ran over and rammed his hand into the narrow void.

"Let's go," Ray said. "Hurry!"

Brody's fingers strained and felt for the gun, but it was beyond his reach. He heard the men coming closer. He had no choice but to leave his rifle behind.

Dashing over rocks and around trees, Brody and Ray

managed to put some distance between them and the men. Mustering the last of his strength, Brody sprinted, pulling Ray along with him, to the spot where the men had made their camp the night before. They paused to catch their breath, look back, and check on the bounty hunters. Both were too preoccupied as they struggled on the loose rocks to look up. The boys slipped behind the boulder at the entrance of the cave.

This time Brody pushed deeper into the darkness, keeping a hand on the wall. He felt Ray grasp his shirt and hang on. "How far can we go?" Brody asked. His voice echoed, as did his panting gasps for breath.

"We have to be quiet," Ray whispered. "It goes a long ways, but I don't have my lantern."

Brody walked slowly, sliding his feet, terrified of falling down a shaft in the floor.

"Let me in front," Ray whispered.

He felt for Brody's hand and then moved it to his rope belt. "Hang on."

Ray moved forward, every now and then whispering instructions: "There's a jag in the rock wall here. Don't cut your hand." "Duck your head until I say okay." "The walls squeeze in tight right here."

The rock walls brushed both of Brody's shoulders. He felt the sensation of a heavy weight pressing down on him, and panic started to bubble up.

"We need to stop a minute," he whispered sharply. He backed up where there was a little more room. His ribs hurt, and he could feel bruises forming from his earlier tumble.

It was truly pitch black in the cave. He waved a hand in front of his face but could not see any movement at all. It was very unnerving. Short of breath, he felt his heart pounding as sweat beaded on his forehead. Unbidden, the panic tried to rise up full-blown. He mentally stomped it back down, desperate not to lose control.

As he calmed down, Brody detected a cool breeze, and it was carrying a strong odor. "Why does it smell funny in here?" he said softly.

"Because of the bats," Ray whispered.

"Bats? Ray, please tell me there is another way out!"

"I have been to the back a few times . . . with a lantern. There is nothing but a small shaft in the ceiling as big as my head."

The pitch-blackness disoriented Brody, and he lost his balance for a second. "We have to get out of here."

"They won't find us," Ray said. "They don't know the cave is here."

Brody put a hand on each side of the passage. The damp stone walls sent a chill into his fingers. "I told you to go home. Why were you down there with the horses?"

"I was on my way to the farm when I saw the horses again. They were still tied to a line in the same spot. Nobody was around, so I thought I would get your buckskin for you. As soon as I went over to it, they came at me."

A voice echoed down the cave passage: "Yooohooo."

"Oh, no," Brody whispered. "Did they find the entrance?" The voices became louder and it worried him that he could hear them so clearly.

"I don't know."

The bounty hunters had not found it the day before. They were close though, Brody was certain of that.

Carl spoke between heaving breaths. "You . . . should"— a groan, and then— "Forget it, I have to rest."

A familiar nasally whine filled the passage. "Hey, boys, are your feet cold?" There was a long pause. "Oh, boyyys . . . are your feet cold?"

Brody wiggled his toes inside his wet boots. His socks were so soaked they made squishing sounds. His heart fluttered, knowing they had left wet marks where they paused on the rocks, leading the men straight to their hiding spot.

He slumped to the ground and leaned against the wall. The very thing he had feared about the cave had happened. He was cornered in the Devil's Den. Reaching up blindly, he found Ray's arm and pulled him close. "Go to the back," he whispered in his ear. "Get back there, now."

Ray hesitated.

"Hurry," Brody said, shaking him by the arm.

Brody let go, and a few seconds later he heard the rustling of clothing snagging on stone as Ray squeezed through the narrow spot.

Brody sat still and collected his thoughts. He sighed, resigned to his fate. He knew he was done for now. All he could do was try to keep them from finding Ray.

After a long while, the passage began to glow. Shuffling stepfalls and cursing voices floated down the passage. The light grew as the men struggled through the narrow places, and Brody could see down the tunnel. The ceiling was dotted with bats, and the floor was coated with old droppings.

A lantern came into view. Lester held it out in one hand, making Brody squint from the brightness. There was a gun in the other. "There ya' are, my bounty boy." He grinned gleefully. "Where's that little horse thief?"

"He left."

"Left?"

"He said he was going for help."

"They ain't nothing gonna help you," Lester said. "Get up. Let's go."

Brody looked away. "I ain't moving. You need to get out of here before people start showing up."

"Shut that sassy mouth and get up!"

Brody stayed.

The glow from the lantern was blocked out for a second as Carl stormed past it, casting an angry shadow over Brody. A strong hand grabbed his hair and jerked him over onto his side. Tiny pops sounded in his head as Carl's strong grip ripped strands of hair from his scalp. It hurt something awful, but Brody was determined not to yell out in pain.

Reaching up with both hands, he grasped the man's wrist. Carl dragged him, yanking hard as he went. When they emerged from the cave, the daylight blinded Brody. He tried getting to his feet, but the man tossed him against the big boulder. The massive stone rested next to the rock wall on one side, forming a dead corner, and the men had him pinned there.

"We got him, Carl!" Lester leaned closer and grinned.

Carl laughed and held his hand up, rubbing his fingers together, letting Brody's ripped hair fall to the ground. "Finally, Lester. Finally." As quick as a rattlesnake, Carl thrust his arm forward, gathering Brody's shirt into his tight fist. He pressed down on him and spoke right into his face, spilling his foul breath everywhere. "I have hunted fifteen men, and you have caused me more misery than any of them!"

"Fifteen," Lester said.

Carl released his grip on Brody's shirt, took a step back, and pointed. "When we get you back to Fort Smith, Billy is going to skin you alive."

"Skin you alive," Lester repeated.

Carl pulled a pistol from his side. "Stretch your legs out in front of you."

Brody pulled his legs tighter against his body, almost in a fetal position. "Why?"

Pointing the pistol at him, Carl commanded, "Now! Stretch them legs out."

"Stretch 'em out, boy!" Lester said gleefully.

Carl glared at the other bounty hunter. "That's enough, Lester."

Brody figured they were going to tie him up. There was some rope on the ground near the lantern. His mind raced. When Lester came to tie him, he aimed to kick him right in the face.

The blow would send him over backwards and right into Carl's legs. It was the only plan he had.

"I'm not going to tell you again!"

Brody pushed his legs out, sliding them very slowly over the ground. He waited for Lester to pick up the rope, but instead Carl moved the barrel of his gun.

"Hold still." He aimed at Brody's feet.

Faster than a lightning bolt, Brody jerked his legs up close to his body. "What are you doing?"

"You are as slippery as anyone I ever chased. You ain't getting away this time, especially with a hole in your foot."

"No! Don't shoot. You're supposed to take me to Billy."

Carl cocked his pistol. "It was Billy's idea to blow a hole in your foot. He said that's what you did to him." Carl made a show of aiming at the spot where Brody's feet had been. "Now, boy."

"Wait!"

"Stick a leg out, unless you trust I'm a good shot." He laughed, and Lester joined him.

Brody panicked and started to roll out of the way, but Carl stopped him quick. "I'll kill you if you try that." Brody froze. "Yep, half bounty if you're dead is better than no bounty if you get away. Ain't that right, Lester?"

"Uh, huh. You is one wiley cuss."

Filled with dread, Brody did the unthinkable. He shoved his foot out, steeling himself for the pain that was about to come.

Chapter Nine

A movement behind Carl caught Brody's attention. His eyes widened in shock to see Wolf standing atop a nearby boulder. He had his old bow pulled tight, with a crooked arrow ready to fly.

Lester saw Wolf, too. "What in tarnation?" he exclaimed.

Carl turned. "Well, looky here, Lester. We got us an old Indian," he drawled.

Lester laughed. "He's going to shoot you with a sharp stick."

Carl eased the pistol around. "You get lost, red man? You ain't in the Territory now. Put that old thing down before it snaps and you hurt yourself."

The bowstring thrummed. In the blink of an eye the arrow seemed to appear out of thin air, sticking out of Carl's wrist. A painful cry erupted from the man's throat. He dropped the gun, fell to his knees, and clutched his wounded arm close to his stomach, moaning.

Lester and Brody looked back, but Wolf was gone as if he had been nothing but a ghost, a figment of their imaginations. Suddenly, he emerged from some brush next to the boulder and had another arrow notched.

"Shoot him, Lester!" Carl screamed from the ground.

Lester fumbled for his gun. It fell to the ground. The Indian walked steadily forward, keeping the bow raised. Lester stumbled back and fell, crawfishing back toward the cave. Wolf lowered his bow. Without pausing, he swiftly drew out a knife and thrust it toward Carl's neck.

"Wait," Brody shouted. "Don't kill him." Although it occurred to him that if that was what Wolf had intended to do, he could have done it with the arrow.

Wolf hesitated. Brody scrambled to his feet, grabbed Carl's dropped pistol, and pointed it at Lester. "Stop moving."

He stepped over to Lester's gun and kicked it down the slope. Wolf moved back and stood with his knife in hand, keeping a watchful eye on the two bounty hunters.

Brody raised his voice. "Ray! You can come out."

Ray came out of the cave, carefully stepped over Lester's legs, and stood behind Brody. For once, he was silent.

Brody alternated aiming the gun at Lester and Carl.

"Get in the cave. Both of you."

"You told us a fib?" Lester looked surprised at seeing Ray.

"Of course he did, you idjit," Carl groaned through clenched jaws. He held his wrist tight around the protruding arrow and struggled to his feet. His red shirt was even redder from the blood smeared on it. A string of foul words spurted out of his mouth.

Wolf retrieved Lester's gun and slid his knife back in its sheath. He gazed thoughtfully at the two men. His stare was more threatening than any hostile words.

Brody centered the gun barrel right on Carl's chest. "Move."

Both men walked slowly to the cave entrance. Carl was leaving a blood trail.

"You just keep digging a bigger hole for yourself," Carl snapped, his face contorted with pain.

"I didn't start this mess. Billy did."

"It don't matter who started it. The Millers will finish it, that's for sure."

"Both of you sit down and cross your legs. Lester, put your hands up."

Lester mumbled something and plopped down, snagging the arrow shaft sticking out of Carl's wrist. Carl roared with pain and collapsed next to Lester.

Lester flinched and whined, "Oh, I'm right sorry about that!"

Carl struggled to a sitting position and punched Lester in the face with his left fist before cradling his right arm again.

Lester clamped his hand over his nose. "Oww, Carl! I said I was sorry!" Blood started streaming between his fingers.

They both looked in such a sad state, Brody almost felt sorry for them. Almost.

The pistol he was holding was still cocked. Pointing it at the ground, he eased the hammer down. "What is Billy going to do with Ames?"

"That black outlaw?" Lester's question was muffled.

Carl just glared, rocking back and forth in pain.

"How did you get Ames to Billy? How long ago?"

Lester had gathered up his shirttail and was trying to rip the bottom off. "I'll tell you if you let us go."

"How 'bout I shoot a hole in your foot to make sure you don't follow me. Then I'll ask you again."

Lester stopped yanking on his shirt. His face was a mess of smeared blood, but Brody could see the dismay in his eyes, nice and clear. "How 'bout I go ahead and tell you. We didn't send him to Billy Miller."

"You have others working with you," Brody said. "Don't lie to me."

Carl choked out a pained laugh. "We ain't never needed nobody else, and we ain't the only ones looking for y'all." He spat in the dirt.

"You are doomed, boy," Lester cackled. "Doomed to die." He had managed to rip his shirttail off and was stuffing the edges up his nostrils, making his voice even more nasal.

Brody stepped back from the cave opening and looked at Wolf. The Indian stared back, unblinking and unfazed by the conversation.

Brody heard a loud snap and a gargled scream. Lester had snapped the arrow shaft off close to Carl's wrist. Carl was pale white but still glaring at Brody. Lester flicked the piece of wood at Brody and grinned, the bloody shirttail hanging from his nose. "We're going to be back on your trail in no time."

Brody felt like he was in a bad dream.

Ray nudged Brody in the side. "You should get out of here."

"No, you should. Go on home and tell your folks to stay away from here for a while."

"I could go get my father."

"No." Brody lowered his voice. "Go home right now. I appreciate your help, but this could mean big trouble for your family."

"You don't know my dad," Ray said.

"No," Brody repeated. "And I mean it. This time go straight home."

"All right," Ray said. He turned and started down the hill.

Brody directed his attention back to the bounty hunters. He had to keep Lester and Carl from following them. Blocking the entrance with rocks would take too much time. He thought about tying them up, but there was not enough rope for both. Killing them would only make matters worse, and his conscience couldn't take it. He needed a way to keep the men inside the cave for a while, a threat that would make them too scared to come out. He had an idea.

He noticed Wolf had tucked the pistol in his waistband, and now held his bow again, nocked with another arrow. "You two sit there and stay put," Brody ordered. "If you get up, or even move too much, Wolf will put another arrow in you."

Brody pointed at Wolf and then pointed at the cave. Wolf nodded. Brody spoke loudly to him. "I'm going to see if the rest of them are here." He knew Wolf wouldn't understand but the statement would surely put doubt in the bounty hunters' minds.

Sure enough, Lester spoke up. "Who you waiting on?"

"The rest of our friends looking for Ames. They have been searching for us since yesterday evening. Wolf worked out our trail and led them here."

"You're lying," growled Carl. His face remained pale from the pain in his wrist, but he still stared angrily at Brody.

Brody glared back. "Am I?"

He made haste down to the bottom and whistled. A whinny carried over the sound of the creek. Brody moved down the stream a ways and whistled again. This time Buck's neigh was loud and close.

He found the horses on a stringer. The bays laid their ears back, and one snapped at him as he untied Buck. Buck snaked his head at it, teeth bared. Brody pushed him back. He rubbed the buckskin's neck, tracing the white scar that ran down it. "Easy, Buck, it's okay. Those poor horses are just like their masters."

Buck impatiently led him to the creek, pulling hard on the reins. Brody felt a surge of anger at the bounty hunters for not taking care of his horse. He bet they had not fed him either.

While his horse drank, he looped the reins over the saddle horn and retrieved a few items from the saddlebag, including his big knife. He left Buck and waded across the stream. At the cane patch he cleaved the tall cane poles at the base with the sharp blade.

After he had felled about a dozen, he tucked as many poles as he could under his arm and dragged them behind him. Buck had finished drinking and was now cropping at the sparse vegetation nearby.

Crossing the stream was easy for Brody, because the cane floated, but the hillside proved more difficult. The ring-shaped ridges on the poles wedged between rocks and stopped him with a jolt. He fell to his knees more than once and was winded by the time he made it back up the mountain. He paused below the cave and laid the cane down, with the ends pointing up the rocky slope.

After resting for a moment, he took half the poles and carried them farther up the hill, placing them in line with the others. Making sure the second bundle overlapped the first, Brody had a row of cane at least thirty feet long.

He found Wolf still standing outside the cave next to the boulder, bow in hand. "Did they give you any trouble?"

Wolf just kept staring at the bounty hunters, giving no indication that he heard Brody talking.

Lester's nasally whine had not been improved by Carl's punch. "That Indian nearly shot me." At least now the rag was not hanging from his blood-stained nose.

"I told you not to come out," Brody said. "I warned you." He cleared his throat in order to produce his best lying voice. "Wolf, our friends are making camp just down the hill."

Carl was sitting, leaned up against the wall of the cave entrance. The gory rag was wrapped around his wrist. He spoke harshly. "Two boys and an old Indian don't make a posse. You don't have anyone else out there. I know a bluff when I hear one."

"There are three more of us. This Indian is going to stay behind too. They sure are a rowdy bunch." Brody saw them look at each other. "They are going to keep y'all pinned up in here until I am long gone. Stay inside unless you want to get yourself shot."

Brody walked out of sight down the hill to the cane bundle and threw leaves and twigs on top of it. The rocky ground was mostly bare, but he managed to find a few dead oak limbs to add to the pile. He went to the lowest end of the poles and lit a match he had retrieved from the saddlebag. The flame ate the dry leaves and twigs, turning them into ash.

Moving quickly, he went up the hill to the point where he could see Wolf but not the cave. He snapped his fingers, and the Indian looked straight at him. Brody motioned for Wolf to come with him. Wolf jumped from rock to rock, moving quickly down the slope. When he passed the smoldering fire, he gave a nod as if he understood Brody's plan.

Down at the creek, Wolf disappeared past the cane patch and into a draw. He returned with his spotted horse. Quickly and efficiently, he used the stringer rope to tie the bounty hunters' mounts, one after the other, to his horse's tail. Brody stored that neat trick away for possible future use.

Wasting no time, he threw Lester's pistol in Buck's saddlebag and turned to Wolf for the other one. Wolf was already on his horse, staring off in the distance. Brody changed his mind about the pistol.

He swung up into Buck's saddle. He wanted nothing more than to go find his Henry rifle, but it was out of reach, way down in the bottom of that crevice. He would come back for it. He chirped to Buck, and they headed along the creek single file.

The first sections of cane exploded from the heat of the fire. The report was as loud as a gun and echoed through the valley. Brody smiled. The flames would creep uphill through the bundle of poles, triggering fake gunshots for at least an hour.

After they had gone a few miles, Brody stopped and went to untie the bounty hunters' horses. Wolf frowned and said something in Cherokee. He wasn't sure if the Indian was upset at him or if he was trying to communicate something else. He kept a nervous eye on the bow, but Wolf did not reach for it.

Brody shrugged. "I don't know what you're saying, but I'm not getting accused of horse theft again." He and Ames had taken some horses from Frank Miller, Billy's son. Although they had paid, the Millers had accused them otherwise. He slapped the horses with the coiled-up stringer, and they snorted and ran, bucking as they went. He held the rope out to Wolf. After a moment, Wolf nodded and reached for it.

They rode another few hours before darkness enveloped the wilderness, forcing them to make camp for the night. Brody started a fire and ate some jerky and old cornbread. The bread had tiny spots of mold, but Brody was so hungry he didn't care. Wolf sat on one side of the fire and stared out into the dark. Brody watched him from the other side. The shadows and flames took turns dancing across Wolf's deeply lined face.

"I sure appreciate you saving me," Brody said. "He was going to shoot me in the foot for sure."

Wolf said nothing.

Brody thought about the challenge that awaited him. He couldn't just ride up to Billy Miller's house without a plan, especially without a gun.

"I lost my rifle." He picked up a stick, pretended it was a gun and took an imaginary shot. "*Pshoo.*" He tossed the stick in the flames. "Gone."

He looked up to see Wolf watching him. The old man held an imaginary rifle to his shoulder.

"Yes," Brody nodded. "Gone. Ames gave it to me, and I've lost it."

Wolf's eyes narrowed. He pointed an angry finger at Brody and then placed his hands on his head as if they were horns.

Brody sighed and shook his head. "No. I didn't kill any buffalo."

"Tla," Wolf said.

"Claw?" Brody asked. He thought that was the word Wolf had spoken, but there was something different about the way he pronounced it. "Claw?"

Wolf grabbed a handful of dirt and held it to his chest as if it were a cherished thing. After a second, he threw the fistful of earth into the fire and pointed at Brody again.

It took a moment for him to understand what Wolf was saying. "I didn't take your land," he said slowly. Brody picked up his own handful of dirt and shook his head before dropping it.

Shadows flickered across Wolf's wrinkled face. His stern expression relayed a long history of strife and broken promises. The deep lines on his forehead and at the corners of his eyes hinted at the countless hours of worry and hardship he had endured.

Momma had taught Brody about the Indians. They had basically been forced off their land, killed while trying to protect what had always been theirs, and promised many things by the government that never came true. That was enough to stir up a whole passel of hate.

"You have the right to be mad," Brody said. "I don't blame you one bit. We had to leave our farm behind, and then the Millers burnt my folks' house. Just about everything we owned is gone. I'm pretty mad about all that, but it don't compare to what you went through."

Wolf shifted and stared at him, making Brody feel the Indian was looking straight through him.

"I cannot imagine how it was for you, but I can promise that not all people are bad. Some of us keep our word."

Wolf shifted his gaze from Brody to the fire. The flames reflected in his eyes, shimmering orange like sunset on a lake. After a few seconds, he spread out his horse blanket, lay down, and turned his back to Brody. The complicated conversation was over, but inside Brody's head it continued. He struggled with a terrible sadness for all that had been done to the Indians, things he had nothing to do with.

Just as he settled down to sleep, a rustle in the brush startled Brody. He was paralyzed with fear, but Wolf leaped up, sweeping his bow and quiver into his hand in the same movement.

A mournful howl pierced the air around the camp.

Chapter Ten

The howl carried on and on before trailing off. Seconds later, four dark shadows shifted around in the edge of the firelight. The wolves' eyes seemed to glow, reflecting yellow, disappearing and reappearing when the animals blinked or moved.

The tiny hairs on Brody's neck rose. Prickles ran over his skin. Grabbing his big knife, he stood and held the blade out. "Get! Get out of here!"

One of the wolves crept closer. It was massive, bigger than any dog he had ever seen. Brody reached for a burning limb in the fire, but Wolf stopped him, putting a hand on his chest as he spoke in Cherokee.

"Why, what?" Brody repeated.

"Why-Ha," the Indian said, pushing gently on his chest.

The Indian lowered his hand and went to the other side of the fire, closest to the wolves. Raising his arms out to his sides, he began to chant.

Brody could only stare in disbelief when the biggest wolf slowly raised its head to scent the air. The hackles on its back lay flat as the soft singsong chant continued. The yellow eyes turned away, and the wolves scattered into the darkness.

After a few seconds, Brody asked, "Will they come back?" He watched the edges of the light, trying to spot the animals. "I've never seen wolves before. That was amazing."

Wolf walked back to his bedding.

"Did you make them go away? Were they scared of us?" Brody knew his questions were worthless to ask, but he couldn't help himself. Just as he was starting to calm down, he heard heavy footsteps rushing toward camp.

"Gotcha!" Carl broke out of the darkness and kicked Wolf, sending him tumbling into the campfire. Wolf rolled out of the flames, leaving a trail of tiny red embers sparkling and spiraling in the air.

Just as Wolf staggered back to his feet, Lester stepped out of nowhere and punched him in the back of the head. Wolf went limp and fell to the ground.

Brody started for his saddlebag, but Lester cut him off. "Is that where you put it?"

Backing up, Brody said, "What?"

"My pistol," Lester said as he grabbed the saddlebag. He reached in to pull the gun out.

Brody saw his chance and took it. He darted into the night and ducked behind a stand of trees. Lester fired, and the pistol belched a plume of orange flames. Staying low, Brody tried to circle the men. Lester shot again and again, until the pistol's hammer clicked against spent hulls.

"Get back here!" Lester yelled. "If you don't get over here, we are gonna kill your Indian."

Brody could see the two men standing in the firelight. Carl stood over Wolf, shielding his hurt wrist with his other hand, yelling at Lester to hurry. Meanwhile, Lester was fumbling for the shells on his gun belt.

Brody did not have time to think, he just acted. He pulled his knife from its sheath and charged toward the bounty hunters.

He had run only a few steps when a huge figure came out of the darkness into the firelight. With no warning, a massive man waylaid Carl with a club-like fist. Brody skidded to a stop in time to see Lester flip the pistol around and— holding it by the barrel—try to hit the man with the handle.

As if swatting a fly, the giant knocked the gun away and wrapped his fingers around Lester's neck. Being at least a foot taller, the man bent low to look the bounty hunter in the eye. "You threatened my boy?"

Brody saw movement on the ground. He slipped closer and reached for Wolf's foot. He pulled. Wolf looked dazed, and he reached up to rub the back of his head. "Get over here," Brody hissed as quietly as he could. He grabbed Wolf's other foot and pulled him back.

"That is the one," Ray said, stepping into the firelight. "He's the one that threw me down."

Carl rolled over, took one look at Ray's father, and then crawled away as best he could.

Lester grabbed at the man's hand. "Let go of me!"

"It don't feel none too good when somebody got ahold of you and ain't gonna let go, does it?"

Lester squirmed and kicked.

The big man reared back, forming a fist with his free hand. "Does it?" He blasted Lester with a blow so hard it knocked him into the dark and out of view. One second he was there, and gone the next.

Everything was silent for a few moments, and then the brush cracked and snapped. Carl said, "Lester, wake your sorry butt up and come on!"

A moan, and then a feeble voice said, "Wait up, Carl, I can't see none too good. There's double of everything."

The big fellow filled his lungs and then bellowed. "You better get, or I'm coming after you'ins!" There was the sound of snorting horses, a few more groans, and then leather slapping horsehide. The hoofbeats quickly receded.

When he turned around, Brody saw the big man's face clearly for the first time. A bushy beard covered his chin, but his upper lip only had half a mustache. "Great goat guts! That was fun!"

Brody backed away, and Wolf stepped right along with him.

"Wait," Ray said. "This is my pa, Eugene."

The towering man stepped over to an old log, picked up one end, and drug it closer to the fire. "Darla! You still toting my bottle?"

"I have it, Pa," a sharp, twangy voice responded.

"Fetch it here." He plopped down on the log.

A skinny girl traipsed into camp. Her beanpole frame made Brody wonder if she had been strung up by her feet when she was a child.

"This is my sister," Ray said. "Her name is Darla."

The girl handed a sloshing corn liquor jug to her daddy. He took it and curled it around, letting it rest on the top of his bent arm. After pulling the cork with his teeth, he raised his elbow and took a big swig out of the bottle.

"Thank you, Mister Eugene," Brody said. He moved closer and offered his hand. "You sure came along just in time."

Even though Eugene was sitting, Brody still had to look up at him. The man lowered the jug, the suction from his mouth making a popping sound as it left his lips. "Whew." His eyes grew wide, and he shook his head. "That'll grow hair on yer chest."

He reached out and engulfed Brody's hand in his calloused paw to shake. Brody noticed that in addition to missing half his mustache, Eugene also only had one eyebrow. His gaze lingered too long, and the brutish man noticed he was looking. He released his grip.

"Stand back and I'll show ya."

"Show me what?" Brody asked.

"Get on back." Eugene took another swig from the jug.

Brody hastened back to Ray.

Eugene leaned toward the fire and spit the liquor into the flames. A scalding hot ball of orange fire rose into the air and quickly burned away. Brody felt the intense heat from six feet back.

"Tried to light my cigar the other night and nearly set myself on fire."

"You were on fire," Darla said. "There was a hole clean through your hat. Don't you remember?"

Eugene laughed, slapped his leg, and took another swig from his bottle.

Darla eased over to Brody's side, tilted her head, and winked at him. "You the man them bounty hunters were after?"

Brody looked from the girl to Ray.

"I told them what happened, and Pa did not take it too kindly."

Eugene's voice roared, "They ain't no man gonna lay hands on my kin, unless they need a whipping, and ain't nobody gonna whip 'em but me." Eugene stood, wobbled for a second, and then took another drink from the bottle. "Ray, get the dogs! We going coon hunting."

"It's too late," Ray said. "We should head on home."

Darla rubbed against Brody's arm. "How'd you get that scar? Were you in a big old fight? Is that why you are a wanted man?"

All of the questions confused him. "Well . . . I . . ." He wasn't sure which question to answer first.

"Can I touch it?" Darla asked. Her fingers were on Brody's head before she finished asking permission. Her examination of his scar quickly spread to include Brody's hair. "It's so soft. Pa, come feel his hair. It's softer than a polecat."

Brody shook his head and shied away from her persistent hands. "I sure do appreciate your help, but Wolf and I should get some rest. I'm in an awful hurry to get to Fort Smith."

"Who is Wolf?" Darla asked, grinning toothily.

"Why, he's . . ." Brody looked around. "Gone. Wolf, where the heck are you?"

"You aren't leaving, are you?" Darla went to her father's side. "Tell him he can't be leaving. I just met him, but he might be the one."

Cocking his head slightly, Brody said, "The one?"

"Let's go wake your ma up," Eugene said, slurring his words slightly. "She should meet Bradley."

"Brody," Brody said. "My name is Brody."

"Right." Eugene burped and looked to Darla. "Ma needs to meet this boy. She knows how to pick a good man."

Darla smiled from ear to ear. "Ma is gonna love him. I just know it."

Brody nudged Ray in the side. "Ray," he whispered. "What in the world is going on?"

"We don't get a lot of company," he said.

"Help me," Brody begged quietly.

Darla grabbed him by the arm, tugging hard. "Come on. I will have to hold his hand, Pa. It sure is dark out there, and the lantern is 'bout tuckered out."

"Well, come on," Eugene said. "Let's see if Ma likes Brady."

With strength far greater than her scrawny arms should have, Darla yanked him to her side. "Stay close so you don't get lost."

"Wait!" Brody said much louder than he wanted.

Eugene stopped mid-swig. "What is it?"

Brody looked to Ray in desperation.

"Dysentery," Ray blurted out. "I forgot to tell ya. Brody has dysentery."

Brody felt Darla's grip loosen. "I sure do," he blurted. "I'm ate up with it."

The girl let go of him and stepped back.

Eugene lowered his jug. "Yer bowels are messed up bad?"

Brody grimaced and clutched his stomach.

"It was awful," Ray said. "The cave we hid in may never be the same."

Brody grunted. "It's getting worse by the minute."

"Maybe we ought to leave him here," Eugene said.

Darla nodded slowly while keeping her eyes on Brody. Reaching over behind the log, she brought a lantern out and lit it.

"Thought it weren't working," Eugene said.

"Oh, I got it fixed."

She looked back at Brody. He quickly doubled over in fake pain, letting out another grunt.

Ray patted Brody's back. "I'm sorry you are feeling so bad."

"Thanks," Brody managed to say, and he meant it.

Darla led the way, with Eugene and Ray behind. "Be careful on your trip," Ray said as they disappeared into the woods.

Brody waited until they had plenty of time to get down the road and then stood straight. Wolf walked out of the dark and back to his bedding, straightened it, and lay down. The corner of Wolf's mouth turned up.

"Huh. Are you smiling?" Brody asked.

Wolf rolled over, his back to the fire.

Brody shook his head and settled into bed. He had trouble falling asleep. Worries of what could jump out of the woods next kept him on edge.

Chapter Eleven

Dawn was breaking when he woke to the sight of Wolf searching the ground around the camp. The Indian kicked branches and leaves aside and then went to his horse and searched the leather packs. Brody wanted to find out what he was looking for, but Wolf saw him watching and stopped.

The Indian reached into a pouch and pulled out something brown. He ripped off a chunk with his teeth and tossed it to Brody. It was jerked venison, smoked and delicious. Brody thanked him, but the Indian had already turned his back and swung up on his horse.

Using sharp motions, Wolf waved Brody over and pointed to Buck. The hard frown on his face told Brody that the grumpy Indian was back and he was ready to go. Brody rolled his bedroll, saddled up his horse, and they left camp.

The ride was silent except for the quick clip of hooves on the rocky ground. This journey in Brody's life was coming to an end soon. He could feel it. To what end and what he could do about it, he wasn't sure. He was just a boy, just one boy.

Brody's frustration made him restless. "We need to hurry. We have to push the horses a little harder."

Wolf turned in his saddle and opened the flap of the leather bag hanging from his horse. He rummaged inside but quickly gave up and turned forward again. Brody started to ask what he had been looking for all morning but then noticed Wolf's knife sheath was empty.

"You lost your knife?"

Wolf looked at him.

Brody pulled his big knife out. "Knife. Did you lose yours?"

He started to put the weapon away but paused. "My grandfather used this one to carve toys for my father. It's been around a long time. My father passed it down to me."

After glancing at the blade, Wolf stared down the road.

"Listen, I know you don't understand, but I can only imagine that your knife was handed down too. I'm sure it meant a lot to you."

Brody rubbed the dark handle, scarred and nicked through several generations of tough, everyday use. "This one sure means a bunch to me. Ames fought a bear with it, probably saved me." He bit his lip, took a deep breath, and then sighed. "I'm headed to jail or worse."

He reined Buck closer to Wolf's spotted horse. Flipping the knife into the air, he caught it by the blade and offered the handle to Wolf. "I would like for you to have it."

Wolf looked at him and tilted his head. One of his eyebrows rose.

"I want you to have it," Brody repeated. "I'm sure it's not as special as the one you lost but . . ."

Wolf stopped his horse, staring hard at Brody.

Brody brought Buck to a halt and watched for a long moment as Wolf's angry face gradually softened. The changes in his chiseled features brought about a peaceful look, as if he had let go of a battle he had been fighting all his life.

Brody eased the knife handle closer. "I really want you to have it."

Wolf reached out, hesitated, and then took the weapon. He examined the knife, turning it over and running his thumb lightly down the blade. When he was finished, he placed it in his sheath and reached into the leather pouch on his horse.

He brought out a long, rectangular piece of cloth. Beads of white and purple were woven into the fabric. The belt was well worn but had no holes. "Wampum," Wolf said. He held the cloth, gripping it tightly for a moment, and then offered it to Brody.

Brody shook his head. "No. You don't have to give me anything."

A bit of anger seeped back into Wolf's face, his mouth forming a hard line. He thrust the beaded fabric at Brody.

Brody reconsidered. He could see no importance in owning such a piece of cloth, but if it would put an angry Indian in a good mood, he would take it with a smile. So he did.

Wolf gave the briefest of nods. He spoke, and then kicked his horse's sides.

"You gnaw lee?" Brody hoped that was a good word.

They rode fast and hard, only slowing to rest the horses twice. As the horses loped on the hard-packed road, an odd feeling came over Brody. He had traveled many miles as a wanted man, ducking and hiding, staying off the road, fearing for his life or his family's.

He did not have any fear or dread now, only determination. It was time to put things right.

Ames was in trouble and he was coming to find him.

They were still a ways from town when they rode out of the woods. The landscape had given way to farming country, and a small house in the shadow of a large barn came into view. Young crops were growing in the garden next to it. Brody caught a whiff of smoke.

A man was rushing about, hurriedly pushing leaves and broken branches into a fire with an old hoe.

Brody pulled up. "Could you tell me where Billy Miller's place is?"

At first, the man barely spared a glance but then took another startled look at Wolf. He paused. "Go down this road several miles. Go past Bill Johnson's old farm. You'll know it by the broken down wagon in the yard. Turn right at the next crossroads. It'll take you to the river valley area. That's where Miller lives."

A woman came out of the nearby barn carrying a rake. She used it to sweep furiously at the ground, sometimes stomping her feet in a bizarre dance. Brody couldn't stop staring.

"Are you headed there to help them?" The man turned back to tend his fire, pushing more brush into it. Buck sneezed as the smoke billowed up.

"Help the Millers? No, sir." Brody gathered up the reins, worried now that these folk might be friendly with the very man that wanted him dead. What if they sent a rider to Billy and warned him that a boy and an Indian were looking for him?

Yet it did not seem to him these folks cared right now who he was or what his business was with the Millers. As they rode away, Wolf kept looking back, mesmerized by the woman's strange dance. Brody glanced back to the man obsessed with feeding the flames that lined his garden. Brody shook his head. These people had lost their minds.

A grasshopper flew into his chest with a buzz, startling him. He flicked it away. Another landed on Wolf's leg, and the Indian slapped it. A few more whirred by, and Brody noticed several were crawling and hopping on the road. It dawned on him that the drone of bug wings had been increasing over the last few moments.

Brody was fascinated. "Wolf, look at all the locusts!"

Wolf frowned and spoke something in Cherokee.

They were only a few in number at first, but the further they rode, the more they increased, until the horses couldn't avoid stepping on them.

"I can't believe this," Brody said, batting constantly at the pests to keep them from landing on his face. "I remember Pa talking about the locusts that would swarm some years, but I never saw so many!" Brody choked and spit when a bug hit him square in the mouth, slapping himself hard while trying knock it away.

Wolf was too busy using his pouch to brush the insects off himself and his horse to notice. Both horses were shaking their heads, and the muscles under their skin would ripple every time a locust flew into them. Their tails were in constant motion trying to whip the bugs off.

They had traveled about a mile when the air came alive with whirring and buzzing sounds. Locusts flew in all directions, and every green leaf and sprig of grass was covered with them.

Eventually, they came to an old abandoned farmhouse dotted with locusts. There was an ancient wagon in the overgrown yard, catawampus on three wheels. The crossroads was just a short ways past it. They turned right.

Brody had hoped to leave the locusts behind, figure out where Miller lived, and then lay low until the evening. Using the night as cover, he hoped to find Ames and get him out without a fight. The locusts were slowing things down.

Going faster was not an option. Trotting the horses was miserable enough, with bugs hitting all of them with loud thwacks, and the drone of the locusts was incessantly thrumming in Brody's ears.

After a few more miles of ducking and dodging the flying insects, Brody noticed trails of smoke rising down the road. They came to a large valley stretching down across low rolling hills in the distance. The smoke and clouds of locusts made the whole scene hazy. The landscape was dotted with people—working, sweating, some tending fires, others raking.

Brody caught sight of a red barn nearby, where two little dark-skinned boys were beating the walls and ground with brooms. The straw in their brooms was stained red with what Brody thought was blood at first, but then he noticed paint cans and wet brushes on the ground. The freshly painted barn walls had ugly streaks where the boys had swatted the insects with brooms.

The area around the aged barn was full of a number of folks of all ages and colors, swatting and squashing the bugs with bundles of switches. Thick quilts had been hung over the doors, and the locusts covered them.

An older man pulled a wheelbarrow full of hoes, axes, rakes, and pitchforks out of the barn and called out. Many of the grown men and women came over, and he handed each an implement.

A tired-looking young woman spotted the two of them on horseback. She came down the path with a firm step, a bundle of switches in her hand. "Did Miller send you to help?"

Brody shook his head. "I'm looking for his house."

A movement caught his eye, and he saw a pale barefooted little girl in a flour-sack dress run up behind the woman. Her blond braids swung out when she peered around the lady's skirt, her eyes wide. Brody guessed she hadn't seen too many Indians.

The woman glanced at her but turned her attention back to Brody. "Keep on down this road. I ain't seen Billy today, but I saw his boy, Frank. Lotta good he going do us. And old Billy is probably drinking sweet tea with his feet up while we out here in this mess."

"I've never seen so many bugs," Brody said, brushing several off of his saddle and legs.

"I think our crops are done for," the woman said grimly, swatting at the bugs whizzing by in the air around her. One landed in the brown strands of her hair. She picked it out and flung it down in disgust. "These hoppers came in this morning and . . . It ain't looking good. Just head on down this road, and you should find the Millers."

The woman was looking curiously at Brody's face. "Say, you look like that boy. You got the scar and all."

Brody broke out into a cold sweat. This was it. There was no turning back. "Thanks, ma'am. We'll be going now. Good luck fighting those bugs."

Brody turned Buck quickly, trusting Wolf to follow. It was all coming to a head, and nothing was going to stop it now. Of course all the people here would know who he was and about the reward posted.

Ames's life depended on him, if he was not already dead.

Brody shied from that thought. He could not bear the thought that the best friend he ever had might be gone.

He had to find Billy Miller's house and wait until the cover of dark. Then he would search carefully until he found Ames and freed him. They would go to Deputy Reeves and tell him the truth about everything—Doc Miller admitting they framed Ames for an old murder, Billy blaming them for Doc's death, and Frank claiming they didn't pay for the horses the night they forced him to give up the ledgers.

Brody felt his anger welling up inside. The Millers were murderers and cheats. They had kept crooked accounts of how much the crops brought in, so the sharecroppers could never pay out their contracts. Though freedmen, they were still slaves to the Millers. Brody's interference in that system just added to the Millers' rage against him and Ames.

They had only traveled a short distance from the farm, when Brody stopped in the middle of the insect-covered road. Wolf looked surprised and sat back in his saddle, halting his horse. The spotted paint shook vigorously. Locusts flew off in all directions.

Brody gathered up his courage. He was not sure how this was going to turn out. "It's time to part ways." He pointed at Wolf, and then back the way they had come. Then he pointed at himself and then down the direction they had been heading.

The Indian frowned and snapped a harsh word at Brody. "Tla!"

"Claw? What does that mean? Well, yell all you want. I don't know what you are saying, and I don't have time to explain. Go find Joseph and Todd. This isn't your fight."

Wolf's face hardened. It was just as Brody had figured. It was not going well. He turned in the saddle to point behind them again, and both of them saw a figure running their direction. It was the little blond-haired girl from the barn. Locusts whirred away from her feet as she ran. When she reached them, she grabbed ahold of Brody's stirrup and asked, "Are you Daniel's friend?"

"Daniel? The stable boy from Fort Smith?"

The little girl bobbed her head.

"Uh . . . yes, I am. Why do you want to know?"

Without a word, the girl sprinted away, up a nearby hill, scaring a whole host of insects into flight as she went.

Brody felt his guts knot up. Daniel must have gotten worse after the Millers shot him. It had happened the same horrible night they had set his parents' house on fire. He wondered how that little girl knew about Daniel.

Looking back to Wolf, Brody said, "Go find Joseph and Todd without me. Tell little Todd that I miss him." He waved his hand toward the road behind them, but Wolf didn't budge. He just continued to stare at Brody and sling his pouch at the bugs.

Frustrated, Brody smashed several on the saddle, leaving a smear of bug guts. "I wish you could understand me. You will end up being one more person the Millers hurt because of me."

Thumping feet got Brody's attention. Three people came running down the hill toward him. The blond girl was leading the way, followed by a skinny black boy and a tall man. The man wore overalls with holes in the knees. Brody recognized Daniel and his father, Noah, right away.

"Brody!" Daniel yelled. His shoulder was still bandaged, his arm in a sling from where the Millers had shot him.

Sliding out of the saddle, Brody's spirits lifted just to see the ever-energetic boy with the huge smile. "Daniel! How are you doing?"

Daniel reached him and slung his good arm around Brody's waist, squeezing tight. "I'm so glad to see you, Mister Brody! I knew you'd outsmart them no-good Millers, just like a fox! And I'm gonna be fine, just fine. We been killing bugs all morning." He hopped around in excitement. "Who's the scary old Indian? He gonna help you kill them Millers?"

Brody grinned. He had missed Daniel's good spirits, bluntness, and nonstop prattle.

Noah shook Brody's hand.

"I'm sorry," Brody said. "I promised I would keep Daniel safe, and I . . ."

"You kept your promise," he said. "You saved him as far as I'm concerned."

"I could have done better."

"He came home still alive because of you, but he sure does use his bad arm for an excuse now. Says he can't be raking locusts."

"Hey," said Daniel. "I been helping."

He lifted one foot and pointed. It was covered in locust guts, legs, and wings. "I stomp those rascals!"

Noah laughed. "Hope you remember to wash those feet off before you go to bed."

Time pressed down on Brody. "Noah, I've got to find Ames," he said. "Do you know where the Millers are keeping him?"

"They took Ames?" Daniel asked, wide-eyed.

Brody nodded. "Billy's got him."

He looked over to Wolf, but the Indian was not there. Brody spotted him by the barn where the boys had been painting. Now the young workers had dropped the brooms down by their sides and were staring at Wolf with their mouths open.

"If Billy got him, he gonna be up at the big house." Daniel pointed. "Up the road 'bout a quarter mile." The little boy came close. "You going up there? You and that Indian?"

Noah scowled. "We been staying clear of his place after what he done to Daniel. They would've had to hang me if I'd come across any of the Millers that night."

Brody did not blame Noah one bit. The Millers had a lot to answer for.

He swept his leather clear of the pests. Before he climbed back into the saddle, he noticed tiny holes in the edges of his saddle blanket where the locusts had been eating it.

"Have you lost all your crops?" he asked Noah.

Daniel's father looked around at the devastation. Locusts

were eating everything they landed on. "It don't look good. Seven years back, I was living in Kansas. I seen this before, only it was worse there, much worse."

"What are you going to do?" Brody asked.

Noah shrugged. "Whatever we can do. Save what we can, replant, and hope for the best. What are you fixing to do?"

Brody paused. "I'm not sure. I'll figure it out when I get there." He looked to Daniel. "Tell Sarah I m-miss her," he stuttered, feeling his ears heat up.

Daniel's eyes twinkled. "Oh, I surely will, Mister Brody," he laughed. "I surely will!"

Chapter Twelve

Brody nudged Buck's sides, but before they could take off, Wolf rode into his path. The Indian's face was streaked with red. His hands were crimson with wet barn paint. The smeared streaks continued onto the bald sides of Wolf's head. He must have raided the hen house, too, judging by the extra feathers tied into his ponytail.

The Indian let out a loud whoop and leaped off of his horse.

That startled Brody. "What do you think you're doing?"

Wolf looked into the sky. "Te-yo-hi!" he yelled. He grabbed his bow and the big knife Brody had given him. "Te-yo-hi." With the bow in one hand and the blade in the other, Wolf began to shout at the top of his lungs and dance. After making a few rounds, he leaped back onto his horse.

Everyone had stopped battling the bugs and was staring at Wolf. Brody finally said, "Umm . . . I guess you're going then, aren't you?"

Brody tapped Buck on the sides, and they trotted out. He tried not to, but he couldn't resist looking at Wolf. The war paint was a sight he was sure many people had not lived to tell about. The whole journey to rescue Ames had become a little unreal.

"There he is!" a worker in a nearby field shouted. "It's him!"

Two women came out onto the road and headed after them on foot. Behind the ladies were Daniel, Noah, and the young girl.

Brody pulled Buck back to a walk. "They're following us," he said to Wolf.

A skinny black man unhitched his mule from a plow and got on its back. He kicked it hard and rode across the fields, shouting. He vanished over the next rise, leaving a trail of dust and swirling locusts behind him.

Brody and Wolf went down a long sloping hill and up another. Looking behind, he could see that more people had abandoned the locust fight and joined the strange parade.

"Stop following!" he yelled back to them. "It's not safe."

The road curved, and after rounding the bend he was amazed to see that the man who had ridden away on the mule was waiting, as were dozens of other people blocking Brody's path. They carried all sorts of farm tools.

"They have the road blocked. I bet Miller ordered them to stop us." Brody didn't see any guns among them, and he and Wolf could easily ride around through the fields, but he hated the thought that Miller was still using these folks to do his dirty work.

As he rode closer, one of the men raised a sharp-looking hoe. Brody started to speak, but the crowd began to part as Buck moved forward.

"Thank you, Mister Brody," someone said. "Daniel said you'd come back."

A few murmured in agreement.

"We can't be living like this anymore," said an old man, gripping a scythe with gnarled hands. "Thank you and your Indian friend for taking a stand."

The man with the mule smiled. "We heard you got Amos and his family free of the Millers."

Brody was shocked. These people expected him to face off with the Millers. He shook his head in protest. "Wait, you don't understand."

A woman stepped out by him and put a hand on his knee. Her eyes were shiny with unshed tears. "They killed my brother because he wanted to leave. They told the law it was a farm accident. We are with you. They got to be stopped." She looked earnestly into Brody's face before falling back with the others.

The ranks closed in behind Brody and Wolf. Chills ran all along Brody's skin at what he was witnessing. These sharecroppers were in the middle of losing their crops—and in doing so, possibly their homes and lives—but now they were coming together to face the Millers. Because of him.

Brody felt as though he was teetering on a cliff's edge. If they went marching up to the Millers' house, people were going to get shot. People were going to die.

Wolf sat tall in the saddle with his chest out and head high. He held his bow lightly in one hand, nocked and ready. The red paint had started to dry and crack on his skin.

The men and women held their makeshift weapons high and clacked them together as they went, while Brody thought furiously. He needed to defuse the situation before the Millers heard them coming.

From behind Brody, one of the sharecropper shouted, "Let's get Miller!"

Brody groaned inwardly, knowing it might be too late to restore calm.

A house came into view. The grand two-story home was stark white with numerous windows and black shutters. A wide veranda stretched across the front with several rocking chairs and low tables. Massive oak trees cast heavy shadows across the fenced yard. A large barn was set back to the side, and all manner of wagons and barrels were around the sides of it. Several other outbuildings could be seen in the distance. In the outlying pasture, Brody could see a large herd of horses grazing. He wondered how a killer with no conscience could live in such a beautiful place.

People pushed through the wide gate that opened up into the yard and pulled on Buck's and the spotted horse's bridles. Surely they made quite a scene, because several workers around the outbuildings and barn stopped what they were doing to stare. One of them jumped on a horse and trotted in their direction.

The men and women behind Brody began to chant, "Miller the Killer!" It was quiet at first but then grew in volume, "Miller the Killer, Miller the Killer!"

Brody imagined Billy had rifles trained on all of them. "Everyone, get back!" he hollered. But the ever-growing group ignored him.

Wolf yelled in Cherokee at the house, shaking his bow and arrow at it. His spotted horse reared up on its hind legs, scattering folk and setting Buck to dancing sideways, ears laid back. Brody felt the danger intensify and the need to do something. He stood up in his stirrups and shouted toward the house. "Billy Miller. Let Ames go! Send him out!"

The group's chant changed. "Send him out! Send him out!"

The door opened. Billy's son, Frank Miller, stepped out. His hair was as red as it had ever been, but his face was redder than Brody had remembered. "You? How could you possibly have enough guts to come here?" He pointed at Brody. "You messed my life up!" He aimed the pistol in his hand.

A sharp-edged hoe spun through the air and crashed against the wall next to Frank's head. At the same moment, Wolf loosed an arrow, whizzing by Frank's side just above his belt. The gun skidded across the porch, and the crowd rushed forward. Hands grabbed, shoved, and yanked.

"Stop!" Frank screamed.

Brody jumped off Buck and pushed his way through the mad sea of bodies until he was face-to-face with Frank. A tall black man with a battered, low-slung hat and a bushy mustache grabbed Frank and held his arms behind him.

"Where is Ames?" Brody demanded.

Frank struggled to free himself. His eyes were wide like those of a wild animal. "Let go of me!"

The air filled with shouts and threats. "String him up! We deserve justice!"

The tall man shook Frank like a rag doll. "Answer the boy."

"I don't know. And I don't care where he is!"

Someone from the group yelled, "Our crops are ruined. We want out of our contracts!"

"We have had enough."

"Tell him, Brody! He can't cheat us no more."

Wolf appeared out of the crowd and shoved Brody's big knife against Frank's chest. Frank felt the blade and ceased struggling. The tall man started to say something, then seemed to change his mind.

"They want out of their sharecropper contracts," Brody said. "It's time you stopped cheating everybody."

"I have nothing to do with these locusts."

"I'm not talking about that," Brody said. "You know exactly what I'm saying. You and your dad have been cheating these folks for years."

Frank's eyes narrowed. "You ruined our lives when you took those ledgers to the judge. You are going to get what's coming to you, you wait and see." He spat in Brody's direction.

Wolf moved the knife up to Frank's neck. The sharp edge pressed against his throat.

"Wait!" His gaze darted to the Indian's painted face. Frank turned several shades lighter. "I didn't mean it. I'm sorry."

"The contracts," Brody said.

"Done," Frank cried. "Done!" he shouted to everyone gathered around.

A cheer went up from those on the porch, and as the word spread, whoops and hollers of joy could be heard.

Daniel trotted up the steps. "I'll go look in that big old house for your friend," he said, and before Brody could stop him, he slipped through the front door. Noah charged after him. "Daniel, get back here! Billy might be in there!"

The woman from the road pushed forward.

"How we gonna make him keep his word?" she shouted, pointing at Frank. "He and his daddy done lied about a killing, he'll lie about this, too. The law don't care none to find the truth. They'll just take his word for it." She spat on Frank.

The cheering died away, and a rumble started up as everyone nodded in agreement. The man towering over Frank spoke up.

"I heard tell of a lawman in Fort Smith that would listen to the truth. He's fair and honors the law."

Brody knew exactly who this man was speaking of. "I've heard of that man." He spoke loudly so that everyone could hear him. "He's the deputy they call Reeves. Ames and I were going to look for him, but the bounty hunters got after us."

The woman shook her head angrily. "Where was this deputy when Billy Miller had my brother killed? No one came to me for the truth."

"I'm very sorry 'bout your brother," the tall man said, ducking his head low. "Word was Reeves went to Indian Territory for almost a year."

Brody turned back to Frank. Wolf had not moved, the knife still firmly at Frank's throat. "What did you do with Ames?"

There was nothing but venom in the gaze Frank locked on Brody. "I didn't do anything with him. I hope he's dead."

Brody struggled with the anguish and rage welling up inside him.

He moved so he was face-to-face with Frank, forcing Wolf to step back. "I am going to ask you one more time, and if you don't tell me, I'm going to let these fine folks with all their sharp objects ask you. Where is Ames?"

"I'm telling you, I don't know." Frank's face twisted into a snarl. "Why don't you go ask my father?"

Daniel and Noah came through the front door. "He ain't there, Mister Brody."

A shot rang out. "Break it up!" a voice yelled. Two men rode up, pointing guns in the air. "Break it up. Everybody get back."

Brody's heart sank when he saw badges on their chests.

One of the men pointed at him. "We're here for Brody Martin."

Bodies shoved and pushed. People shouted. "No! Brody stays with us!"

One of the lawmen fired into the air again. "Back away!"

Frank took his chance. He threw his head back, catching the man holding him right in the mouth, and tore free. He ran straight into Wolf, knocking him backwards off the porch. Brody was powerless to stop Frank from running for the barn, but Wolf shot to his feet and took after him.

Brody ran down the step to give chase, too, but a large black woman grabbed him in an iron grip and pulled him close. "Leave this boy alone," she bellowed at the deputies. "He saved us from the Millers." Several voices joined hers in agreement.

A strong hand grabbed Brody's shoulder. It was the tall man, the one who had restrained Frank. He tore Brody free from the woman and pulled him through the bodies surrounding them. The woman came after both of them, but the man smiled over his shoulder at her and, said, "I got him, I'll keep him safe." She hesitated. The big man did not stop.

He bent low, guiding Brody through the press of bodies. The deputies were still yelling, the sharecroppers shouted, and weapons were being brandished on both sides. Someone was going to get shot.

They slipped out from the crowd by the side of the house. A horse was there, and the man made a beeline for it. Brody tried to pull back, but the man's grip was too strong. "Hey, I've got to find Ames!"

The man grabbed him around the waist and flung him into the saddle. Before Brody could comprehend what was happening, the man pulled himself up behind him, grabbed the reins, and they were off across the yard behind the house.

"No! Let me go!" Brody said in dismay. "I have to go back and get Ames." He kicked and squirmed, but the big man's arms were around him like a steel trap.

They were galloping down a little track that ran the length of the pasture fence. Locusts flew up and pelted him. They were getting further and further from the Millers' house. They were getting further from Ames.

"Let me go," Brody demanded. He reached for the reins, but the man hooked his arm around Brody's, pinning them. Brody struggled, until the man leaned close and said, "You want to see your friend again, you better be still."

Brody's heart sank. This man was no sharecropper.

Brody sat rigid in the saddle, trying to understand what was happening. The man had slipped him away from the deputies, and by his actions Brody knew he was not a friend to Frank. What did that leave? A man that had grabbed an opportunity to get a bounty.

Bounty hunter.

If this man was taking him in to collect his bounty, then that meant he was being taken to Billy, and Billy had Ames.

Somehow Brody had to find a way to get them out of this. *Or,* he thought grimly, *I'll die trying.*

Chapter Thirteen

As they left the fields behind, no more locusts flew into his face. The buzzing of their wings was gone. Brody smelled honeysuckle and privet hedge blooming. It reminded him of their old farm. He desperately longed for the old home place, where we had lived before he knew about being hungry, before bears and bounties and killers.

He yearned for those moments that brought him through his worst times. Momma throwing her head back in laughter at his and Papa's antics, and even working the crops with Papa, knowing they would come back to a table full of good food and soft beds. Mostly, he ached with his whole being for those moments in the evening, safe and loved, in a home filled with family.

The horse broke stride to avoid a large rut in the path, jolting Brody back to his current predicament.

The track they were on emptied out onto the main road. The man's horse raced as if his life were on the line, making several miles pass quickly. Soon the way opened up, and Brody could see houses close together. There were more wagons on the road, and the man pulled his horse back to a trot. They topped a small rise, and Brody realized they were heading into Fort Smith.

"Hey, where are you taking me?" he asked. The man did not bother to answer. Brody was flummoxed. Was Billy Miller hiding in town?

The streets of Fort Smith went by in a blur, as did the people on the boardwalks. He tried to focus on some of the faces, mortified at the thought of Sarah seeing him in this most undignified position. Several people stared, and a few laughed and pointed. Brody felt his ears burning and turned to look straight ahead.

The man guided his horse down several streets. Finally, he stopped by the side of a large two-story brick building. Several men came out of a door, and one grabbed the horse's bridle. The horse huffed in deep breaths, sending foam flying off the bit in his mouth

The black man climbed off and headed toward a door in the building, rubbing his sore mouth where Frank had head-butted him. "Get down," he said over his shoulder.

"Good work, Bass," someone called after him. "They're waiting on the boy now."

A second man reached to help Brody down, but Brody glared at him, making him raise his hands and back off. Brody swung down out of the saddle.

The man was dressed in a fine suit and smelled of sweet tobacco. His face was pale, and his palms looked soft as he swung a hand out toward the door and inclined his head. "Very well, then . . . this way, young man."

After going through a couple of doors and a short hallway, they entered a well-lit room with a big desk and four leather chairs. The man motioned for him to take a seat. Brody slid into the chair and looked around. The desk was piled high with papers, neatly stacked. A pen and inkwell sat on the blotter, and Brody caught his breath when he saw what was next to them.

It was the WANTED poster Billy Miller had put up around town, accusing Ames and Brody of murder and horse theft.

Brody slumped down in the big chair, defeated.

The man in the suit noticed Brody's despair and apparently felt an inkling of mercy at the state of his charge. He went to a stand and poured water from a pitcher into a small glass. He came back to Brody and held it out.

"Here. You look a bit peaked, and I imagine you are tired, hungry, and thirsty, given what I have heard about today's events. I cannot do anything about the former two items, but water I have."

Brody nodded. "I'm so hungry my legs are shaking, but water will do just fine." He mumbled his thanks between slurps. It was tepid, but good. His thirst overwhelmed him, and he drank the rest down.

"Good," the man said with approval. "I am the deputy court clerk today, so you have the pleasure of my company for the moment."

He took the glass and put it back by the pitcher. He glanced over at Brody and walked to the door they had come through. "Stay put."

As the man reached for the door handle, the door opened and the deputy they called Bass walked through. The farmer clothes were gone, and he was shrugging a jacket on over his shirt and vest. Brody could not look away from the badge that hung prominently on the left side. "We cut it a little close, didn't we?" Bass said to the man in the suit. "I'll let the commissioner know he's here."

"You did a fine job, Mister Reeves. A fine job indeed." The deputy clerk walked to another door across the room and opened it for him.

Reeves! Brody sat up straight. This was the man Joseph had wanted him to speak to. "Wait," he said, but Bass Reeves had already gone through the doorway that opened into a long hall with seats along one side.

Brody could see Reeves as he walked down the hall, opened another door, and waved a hand at someone inside. "We need you back in there." A man limped into the corridor and followed him.

Brody was overcome with excitement. *Ames!*

He jumped to his feet and ran across the room. The deputy clerk swiftly stepped in front of him and closed the hallway door, tense and ready. "There's no need for that."

"But that was Ames!"

"Go sit down, Mister Martin!"

Brody glared at the man. The man stared back, unmoved. This guy dealt with belligerent outlaws everyday, and an upset fifteen-year-old kid did not seem to bother him in the least.

Brody turned and walked back to his chair, his mind racing. He was beginning to realize the bounty hunters had never had Ames. Nor did Billy. The law must have caught Ames too, but at least he was alive!

The clerk relaxed and adjusted his tie. "It won't be long. You'll go before the commissioner next."

It wasn't clear to Brody who the commissioner must be. He guessed it had to be a fancy name for Judge Parker. The judge had hung many men, and Daniel, the stable boy, had told Brody about a ten-year-old boy who had been sentenced to death. The image of the judge slamming his gavel down came to Brody's mind. *You will hang by the neck until dead.* He shuddered.

The deputy clerk stepped over and reached toward his head. Brody flinched.

"Don't be so jumpy, boy." He pulled a dead locust from Brody's hair, threw it in a trash can in the corner, and walked to his desk.

Brody rubbed his sweaty palms against his britches. Since he entered the courthouse he had been smelling a faint odor without being fully aware of it, but now it permeated the room. It had become strong enough that he fought the urge to pinch his nostrils.

The man sat at his desk, folded a sheet of paper, and fanned it in front of his face. "It's seems worse today than it's been in a long while."

"What is it?" Brody asked.

Pointing at the floor, the man said, "The jail."

He looked down. "The jail?"

The deputy clerk set his paper fan on the desk and chuckled. "There are at least a hundred men down there crowded together, all using the same buckets. Some have been there for months, and none have had a bath during that time. I don't know how they manage to breathe at all."

A lump formed in Brody's throat. He had heard of the dreaded Fort Smith jail. One big room, with murderers and petty thieves all shoved in together. Just spending one night in there could be a death sentence. Men headed for the hangman's noose had nothing to lose and would kill just to be entertained.

Sweat beaded on his forehead. His palms grew clammy.

There was a knock on the hallway door. It opened, and a bald man leaned inside. "He'll be ready for the boy in a moment."

"We will be right there." The door closed, and the clerk crooked a finger at Brody.

Brody glanced in the direction they had come from. Every muscle in his body tensed. *I could make a break for the door.*

The deputy clerk gave Brody a hard look and then tilted his head toward the hall. "It's time. Let's go."

Standing slowly, Brody's legs shook as the strength left them. It was time to get it over with, time for the end of all this mess.

Chapter Fourteen

The corridor was empty, and the sound of their steps echoed down the hall. A murmur of voices became louder and louder as they approached a double set of doors. A sharp pop sounded three times. One of the doors opened, and the volume of the voices tripled.

Brody tried to peek inside, but the deputy clerk was blocking his view. The sharp popping sound repeated. "This is the last warning," a clear deep voice said. The chatter grew quieter. "Everyone will be escorted out if need be."

The clerk bent close to Brody's ear. "This is not how it's normally done. Young man, you have turned everything upside down." He placed his hand on Brody's back and pushed him into a big musty room.

Large windows at the front of the room were wide open, but it did little to thin out the rank odor of the prisoners in the basement jail. There were rows of chairs in the middle of the room and an aisle down the middle. Sections of chairs also ran along the side walls. All the seats were full of people, and many more observers stood at the edges of the room and behind a wooden rail at the back.

Deputy Reeves came over and took his arm. He walked him down the aisle between the chairs and benches all the way to the front, stopping near a large desk on a raised platform.

An individual with a stern expression on his face sat behind the desk. Brody figured this had to be Judge Parker, the man who could have him hanged.

A short fellow with thick glasses came up to him, took ahold of his hand, and placed it on a Bible. "Do you swear to tell the truth, so help you God?" The man had a broad mustache, and with every word spoken, the ends of it wiggled.

Brody hesitated.

"Well, do you?" the man demanded.

Someone in the crowd coughed loudly. Reality hit Brody in the pit of his stomach. Everything was happening so fast. He was on trial!

He licked his dry lips and struggled to find his voice. "I do."

Reeves bent low and started talking to the judge, but Brody could not focus on his words, because over the deputy's shoulder, he saw Billy Miller sitting at one of the tables.

Miller's unshaven face was red, his eyes hard as stones as he looked at Brody. Matching him stare for stare, Brody felt his rising anger burning away much of his fear.

Reeves turned and blocked Billy from his view. Brody took a look around the stuffy room and realized just how many folks were staring at him.

In the crowd, he found familiar faces, each one taking his emotions on a wild ride. His parents were near the front, with Todd sitting between them. Upon seeing him look their direction, Momma leaned forward and mouthed silently, "Love you, Son." Her hands were wound tightly around one of Todd's.

Todd grinned and waved with his free hand. "Hi, Flint!" Momma hushed him. Before the truth came out, Brody had told Todd and Joseph his name was Flint.

Papa tried to give him a reassuring smile, but Brody also saw the dark circles under his eyes. Mary was sitting behind them, looking worried. She caught his eye and turned to look pointedly at the north wall.

Ames was standing there stiffly, eyes wild and darting. Brody feared he was lost in his mind again, back in the battle that happened on the Devil's Backbone so long ago. A deputy was standing just a few feet away from him, thumbs hooked in his gun belt.

Brody was grieved that he had brought Ames to this, and that his family and friends would now witness his own trial and accusations. Most of all he felt sorrow that his family would hear the gavel fall and the judge announce his fate.

A hand touched him on the shoulder. Bass was looking at him, and Brody thought he detected sympathy in his dark eyes. "I said, you need to sit down." He pointed to a chair on the platform behind him. It was just to the right of the judge's big desk.

Brody swallowed hard. "Sorry, sir." His gut knotted. He felt sick, but somehow he managed to sit without throwing up. The chair was facing the crowd, giving him a better view of the people.

Eli Miller was sitting near the front. Billy had forced Eli into tricking Brody and leading him into an ambush. Even so, Brody had made peace with him after giving him a stiff right hand. His black eye had faded to dull blues and browns. Brody couldn't help but wonder if his one-time enemy still had eyes for the beautiful Sarah.

The doors at the back of the room burst open. Some of the sharecroppers, still carrying their tools, rushed inside. Brody recognized a woman in the front. She had tried to shield him from the lawmen at the Millers' farm. "Let him go!"

A deputy rounded on them. "Hey, you can't come in here!"

Daniel popped out from behind the woman, shouting, "You let Mister Brody go! He done saved us from Miller the Killer!"

Daniel's father shoved out of the crowd and grabbed Daniel. "Son, you best get back here. Your mama will tan your backside and mine, too, if she finds out you in here!"

Brody felt his spirits lift a bit at the sight of his young friend trying to stand up for him. Daniel's father dragged him out of sight, but everyone could still hear him yelling about Miller the Killer. The crowd began to rumble, and some folks in the front stood up to get a better view. The judge on the raised platform pounded the table with a wooden gavel, shouting for order.

Deputy Reeves said something to the judge, who quieted for a moment to listen, then nodded. The deputy gently moved folks out of the way, until he reached the sharecroppers. He spoke softly to the group, but Brody could not make out his words over the voices of everyone else.

Hands waved. Fingers pointed. Finally, the sharecroppers retreated to the back and allowed Bass to take their hoes and rakes out of the courtroom. Everyone was still talking at once.

The sound of the gavel cracked across the room. "There will be quiet in this courtroom!" the judge roared. Silence descended, and the only noises left were the creaking of chairs and the rustling of clothes.

The judge harrumphed and straightened the papers on his desk. "That's better. Now let's get this over with." He turned to Brody. "Brody Martin?"

Brody nodded.

"Brody, my name is Stephen Wheeler. I need you to answer some questions."

"Wait . . . you are not Judge Parker?"

"I'm the commissioner. The judge will hear the case if there's no guilty plea. Let's get started."

Relief flooded Brody's body. He took a deep breath. "Yes, sir."

Commissioner Wheeler moved a sheet of paper on the desk and looked at some scribbled notes. "In November of last year, did you come in contact with Gordon Miller?"

"Gordon?" Brody asked.

"He usually went by Doc Miller."

"Yes, sir. I met him in Fort Smith."

Commissioner Wheeler wrote something on the paper. "Tell me about it, from the beginning."

"The beginning?"

"How did you come to meet Mister Gordon Miller?"

Brody glanced to his parents. "Our farm was in a bad way, with the drought and all. Me and my folks were going hungry, so they wanted to move and I did not, so I snuck out to go hunting at the base of a mountain ridge called the Devil's Backbone. I was careless and had me a bad accident, and it blinded me for a while."

"Is that where your scar came from?"

Brody traced the scar with his fingers. "Yes, sir."

"Continue."

"Well, Ames—"

"Ames, also known as Amos, with no known surname?"

"Umm . . . yes, sir."

"I see. Continue."

"As I was saying, Ames . . . uh . . . Amos found me and took care of me 'til I could see again. The war was over, but he still thought it was going on."

"He was unaware the war was over? How on earth . . ."

"Well, he was a bit confused and tried to shoot me one night during a thunderstorm"—Brody heard his momma gasp, and the judge's mouth opened, so he rushed to finish—"but he did not mean it! He took real good care of me other than that . . . well, mostly." He let his voice trail off, remembering.

Are ye Union, or Confederate? Brody would never forget staring down the barrel of that gun.

Brody saw the deputy near Ames step a few feet further from him. Ames was looking down at the floor and did not notice.

"When I was better I went home, but my folks were gone. I thought they were dead from starving. Ames showed up later, and we had a big bear stalking around the cabin."

The commissioner's eyebrows rose. "A bear?"

"Yes, sir. It broke in and we fought it."

Mister Wheeler leaned forward. "You two fought with a bear, inside your home?"

"It was something terrible," Brody said.

"I imagine so. What happened next?"

"It knocked me against the wall, and Ames stabbed it with a knife in the back, but it just got madder."

Mister Wheeler dropped his pencil. "He stabbed a bear in the back?"

"Yes, sir. I loaded my grandpa's old musket and—"

"Hold it." The commissioner held his hand up. "Hold on. I have gotten us off track. It is a fine and superbly interesting story, one I truly would like to hear the full course of, but I need at this moment to know about Gordon Miller."

"Well, sir, I am coming to that," Brody stated. "Ames got hurt pretty bad by that bear, so I had no choice but to go for help. I met Doc . . . uh, Gordon Miller in Fort Smith. He said he could help my friend, if I promised to pay him to come and help."

"And did he help him?"

"No. He came to the farm but wouldn't help. He tried to rob me and kill Ames."

Wheeler flipped to another sheet of paper. "Tell me about that."

"I heard Doc Miller talking about him and his brother, Billy, killing some people and blaming it on Ames."

The crowd broke into chatter. Wheeler looked up and glared. He waited for a moment, and the room quieted. "What happened after that?"

"We had a scuffle, and Doc tried to run Ames over with his horse and buggy."

"And?"

Brody began to speak but the wind left him. "I . . ."

"Go on." Wheeler picked his pencil up.

Brody glanced at Ames. The big man looked back and nodded. "I waited as long as I could," Brody said. "I couldn't shoot a man, so I shot his horse." His stomach twisted at the memory. "It all flipped over into a big mess. . . ." Brody bit his lip. Finally, he said, "Doc was killed. I killed him, but I didn't mean to."

He dare not look at Momma. He knew she would be crying.

Wheeler's expression remained unchanged. "About a week later, did you come in contact with that man?" Wheeler pointed to a rotund black man sitting at a table near Billy Miller. The man looked familiar, but it took Brody a minute to recognize him without his tall hat.

It was Preacher, the man who was helping the Millers fool their sharecroppers into staying under contract.

"Preacher," Brody said. "He don't have his big hat on, but his name is Preacher."

"His true name is Walter Ware. Did this man you know as Preacher tell you how to find the Millers' farm?"

"He was helping the Millers cheat his sharecroppers."

Commissioner Wheeler laid his pencil down. "Please answer the question asked of you."

Brody nodded. "Not really," he said. "We were looking for Ames's family. We found them at Frank's farm, so we never made it to Billy's."

"You're speaking of Frank Miller, Billy's son?"

"Yes, sir," Brody answered.

The commissioner looked at him. "The night you were at Frank's would have been in December of last year. Correct?"

Brody knew what was coming: the accusation of horse theft at Frank's place. The penalty for that would be nearly as severe as the one for Doc Miller's death.

Brody stood and faced the audience. Though it was hard to do, he looked straight at his family.

"What are you doing, young man?" Wheeler asked. "Sit back down."

"I'm going to make this easy," Brody said. "I caused Doc Miller's death. If I had not shot his horse, he would still be alive. I took the horses from Frank's farm too. You can let Ames go. I did it."

Chapter Fifteen

The people around the room broke out into a chattering of voices. Momma was wiping tears from her face.

The commissioner grumbled as he sorted through the papers on the desk. At last he said, "Aha!" and held up a sheet. He ran his fingers along the writing, and then slapped a hand down, making Brody jump and everyone else quiet down.

"Now see here, Mister Martin. Your friend, Amos, told me that money was left in exchange for the horses."

Brody looked Wheeler in the face, "It was, but we can't prove it."

"It wouldn't matter if you could," Wheeler said. "You can't force a man to sell his property."

Brody glanced back toward his folks. "You're right." He paused. "I'm ready."

"You're ready for what?" the commissioner asked.

"I'll plead guilty if you leave Ames alone. He doesn't deserve this. He's saved my life so many times, even saved me from a wildman in the territory."

"A wildman?" Wheeler asked, astonished.

"He was killing folks and taking their supplies."

"Killing people?"

"He had fur pelts all over him, looked like an animal and acted like one too. He had these long knives and would—"

"That's enough, young man." Wheeler shook his head in disbelief. "We will have to discuss this, er, *wildman* at a later date. Let's stick to the current events, please."

Brody nodded. "Yes, sir. I've pled guilty. You can sentence me when you're ready." He waited for the words that would send him to the gallows. Shame kept him from looking at his family.

Commissioner Wheeler took a deep breath before he spoke. "While there are matters that we will need to discuss, some of which you brought up today, we are not here about you." A few people started to murmur, but a stern look from Wheeler shut them down.

"Not here about me?" Brody looked at his mother and father. Momma managed a weak smile. Papa looked solemn, but then he winked. "I'm confused," Brody said.

"I have one more question," Wheeler said. "While you were at Frank's, did you find these papers and ledger books?" He indicated a small table in front of his desk. On it were the familiar books he had taken from Frank Miller's house.

"Yes."

"And did you see that these items were delivered to the courthouse?"

"I did. I had Daniel, the stable boy, bring them here."

"And who shot the bullet that made a hole nearly all the way through the books?"

Brody turned to Billy Miller and pointed straight at him. "He did, when he tried to kill me at the Crawford County crossing."

An angry rumble came from the spectators in the courtroom. "Hang Miller!" several of the sharecroppers shouted, followed by murmurings of agreement all around.

The commissioner and the deputies shouted for order. Bass Reeves called for silence, and at last the room settled.

Wheeler gathered up some papers. "I am finished with you."

"But . . ."

"Sign this statement, and go sit with your family."

Applause broke out. People shouted.

"Stop that! Hold it down!" Wheeler ordered.

Brody signed the paper and, with weak legs, stumbled off the platform. His family wrapped their arms around him. Momma pulled him down, making him sit beside her. Todd hugged him tight.

Ames limped over to sit by Mary. The wrinkles on his face

were deeper, and he looked tired to the bone, but he leaned forward to clap Brody on the back. "Ye done fine, li'l fella."

After the room quieted back down, the commissioner turned toward the table where Billy Miller and Preacher sat.

"Billy Miller, the evidence brought forth cannot be denied. You have been accused of murdering Mrs. Brown at her place in Crawford County and framing the man known as Amos, or Ames." The commissioner looked down at the paper in his hand.

"You have also been accused of selling land across the border in the Territory—land that was not yours to sell." He gestured to the left side of the room. "These people are just a few of the families now homeless because of you."

Standing solemnly against the wall were a redheaded man and a worn-out looking woman hanging tight to his arm. The man had two jagged stripes that scarred his face and one milky eye. Brody remembered them as some of the squatters he had witnessed being forced out of Indian Territory.

"You will also face charges of arson, assault, and the attempted murder of the stable boy, Daniel. I'll also advise you there are more charges to come, but today we are only addressing the first two I mentioned, murder and falsifying land contracts. To these charges, what is your plea?"

Billy Miller stood, sweat drops standing out on his forehead and wet spots at his armpits. He glared unwaveringly at Brody. "Not guilty."

The commissioner gathered the papers on his desk and motioned to Mister Reeves. "The evidence in this case will be presented to a grand jury on the seventeenth of May. You will have opportunities to meet with your counsel, but for now you will be held without bail."

The crowd cheered as the deputy marshal bolted an iron cuff on Billy Miller's wrist. His face turned a deep red, and he yanked his other hand back into a fist and swung.

Reeves dodged the swipe and pulled the cuffed hand up

behind Miller's back. The man spat awful curse words and thrashed around in a circle. It took several deputies to take him to the floor and get the other cuff on him.

"You can't send me down into that putrid hole! I was a deputy here! Those murderers will kill me!" he bellowed.

Wheeler shouted, "Get him out of here!"

Reeves and another deputy heaved Miller to his feet and hustled him out the nearest door.

When Wheeler turned back to face the courtroom, he had to shout to be heard. "Those of you who were questioned will receive a writ to appear in court if this goes to a jury trial. Everyone is dismissed. Please exit out those doors, and good day."

The room exploded into a loud buzz of voices as people stood up. Momma had an iron grip on Brody's arm, as if she thought he was going to disappear again.

Papa said something to him, but it was so noisy that Brody couldn't hear what he said. Leaning closer to Brody's ear, he spoke loudly, "Let's go outside." He tapped Ames on the shoulder and pointed toward the doors. Ames nodded and looked to Mary, but she was several rows over, talking to one of the sharecropper women. Ames shrugged and led Papa toward the doors. Brody followed behind him, his mother hanging on to him and Todd holding onto his shirttail.

When people saw him leaving, the noise became more celebratory. Hands of all sizes and colors patted Brody and Ames on the back. As they reached the doorway, a hearty round of applause broke out.

Just outside the doors stood Joseph. He smiled widely at Brody, but before he could say anything, a small figure leaped up at him. "Pop!" Todd squealed.

The big Cherokee caught Todd in mid-leap. "Little cub!" Though Todd was small for an eight-year-old, he had a huge personality. He was already poking his father, pulling on his nose, and laughing.

Brody watched their reunion while Momma pulled him against her side, tears once again falling unheeded down her cheeks.

Brody fought back his own tears of joy. He had never been so proud, so happy and relieved to have his life back and to reunite Todd with his father. Ames shook hands with Joseph while Joseph thanked him for his help finding Todd. Papa introduced himself and Momma and then began telling Joseph about how the events had unfolded in the courtroom.

"Where's Sarah?" Brody asked Momma.

"Her father would not let her come."

"Oh. He still doesn't want me talking to her?"

Momma looked to Papa. "I suppose not."

Mary came out with some other ladies. She walked up and hugged Ames. "Finally. That old devil finally got what was coming to him."

Ames hugged her back, hard. "Mary, that road leading here were a hard one, but we done with it."

Papa placed his hand on Brody's back. "Let's get in the wagon."

"Where we going?"

Momma clasped her hands together. "Some people from the church are bringing some food over to the farm." She turned to Ames. "We would love for you and your family to come."

Mary said, "Thank you, Miz Martin. That'd be right kind of you folks."

Joseph ruffled Todd's hair, causing him to grin and wiggle to get down. Joseph laughed and turned him loose, and he made a straight line for Momma.

She crouched down to his level. "And you have to come," Momma said. Todd threw his arms around her. "Yes!"

"It's a pleasure to meet you, by the way," she said, rising up to shake Joseph's hand.

Papa shook with Joseph, too. "Todd has been like a second son to us."

"Thank you," Joseph said. "Thank you for keeping him safe. I rode out to your old place and found it empty. Some people on the trail told me news of Billy's arrest. I hoped I could find you here."

There was a commotion as Wolf rode up through the stragglers still hanging around. Several voices shouted, "Watch it!" or "Hey, look out!" but the Indian was oblivious. Buck was tied to the tail of Wolf's horse. He stopped just beside them and slid deftly out of the saddle and to the ground.

"Buck!" Brody and Todd yelled at the same time. The buckskin threw up his head, ears pointed forward. He whinnied loudly and bumped into Wolf's horse. Before Brody could untangle himself from his mother, Todd was already there, working the knot loose, talking nonstop to Buck.

Brody started to thank Wolf for bringing his horse back when the ever-curious Todd trotted up to the Indian and stopped in front of him. Buck halted just behind Todd, nibbling at the boy's hair. Todd stared up at this strange man, and the strange man frowned back at him.

"Do you know you got a lot of red paint on your face?" Todd asked seriously.

Wolf frowned so hard at Todd that Brody thought his wrinkles were going to crack right along with the dried paint.

Joseph let out a great boom of laughter, and Brody found himself joining in. Soon everyone was chuckling, except Wolf. He looked at Joseph and Brody, then down at Todd. He folded his arms and stared off into the distance. That sent both of them off into another burst of uncontrollable laughter.

"This is Joseph's father, Wolf," Brody finally explained, when he caught his breath. "He saved me when the bounty hunters had me trapped in a cave."

"Brody Martin," Momma drew up in shock, "My heart can't handle any more news like that today. Please!"

He felt a stab of guilt at what she had had to hear in the courtroom. Momma placed both hands on either side of his face. "My Brody-boy. It is so hard to see you as a young man, one that has survived so much, and now you've come back to us."

"I know, Momma, but I am back for good. It is all over. Can I please just be your son, now? No Millers or marshals?"

Momma laughed and pulled him in tight. Brody felt contentment course through him. He was with his family, and his family was his home.

Momma turned him loose and looked up at Joseph. "Please come to our home, and bring your father too. Our home is . . . was at Massard Prairie. You can follow us there."

Joseph looked over at his father. Todd had reached up and was rubbing the flaking paint off of Wolf's arm. Wolf looked off to the horizon. "This war has been won. It is time for families to come together," Joseph said.

Chapter Sixteen

Brody arrived first, riding on Buck. His parents' farm was pretty much the way he remembered it . . . burned to the ground by the Millers.

Wooden timbers had been reduced to nothing more than a pile of blackened sticks with streaks of white ash. Parts of the porch remained, and the bottom two steps were nearly intact. Though it had been many days since the fire, tiny wisps of smoke rose from the rubble.

His parents had a large canvas tent in the front yard. A make-shift table sat next to it with long boards sitting atop wooden sawhorses.

Papa helped Momma down from the wagon just as everyone else started to arrive. Joseph and Wolf went to the well and drew a bucket of water up to wash. Joseph and his father talked, while Wolf tried to rub the red paint from his skin. Todd had managed to untie Buck and was plucking grass for the horse to eat. Brody saw Joseph motion to Todd several times as he talked, and each time his father shook his head in answer. It did not look like the conversation was going too well.

Ames arrived on his old mule with Mary doing her best not to slide off. "Slow down, Amos." She clung to his shirt, pulling it tight against his neck.

Brody helped her down.

While smoothing her clothing, she said, "I'm way too old to be riding double."

Ames climbed down. "You done fine."

"Ames," Momma scolded. "You're not planning on riding double back to Crawford County, are you?"

"No," Mary said quickly. "I rode his old mule to Fort Smith yesterday. I'm still sore from that." She laughed. "This short ride today nearly done me in. I'm glad Amos has a wagon lined up for us."

"You could borrow Buck," Brody said.

Ames patted his mule on the neck. "One of them sharecroppers done offered up the use of his wagon. He live just over the river."

"But I don't care for you using Buck. Mary could ride him."

Leaning close, Ames said, "She ain't wanting to ride. She think she need a seat and a big old fluffy pillow."

Mary slugged him in the shoulder. "You better hush."

Ames chuckled and led his mule over to a fence post to tie him. Momma and Mary walked away, both laughing. Brody's heart was full of joy as he watched all of this unfold.

The sound of laughter, the bright blue sky, the warm day—everything seemed perfect until a stray breeze carried a faint whiff of smoke. He turned back to the burned house and wandered over to what was left of the old porch steps.

Ames joined him. "Sure were a great big bunch of folk at the courthouse."

"I don't know if I have ever seen so many people in one place. Where are Anna and Luke?"

"Mary said Anna ain't feeling real good. Luke stayed with her."

"Reckon once that baby comes, everyone will be feeling better." Brody plucked a blade of singed grass.

"I done put her and Mary through a world of trouble."

Brody glanced at his Momma. "We both put the folks we love through a lot."

"I sure did think I were done for when them deputies took me. Just knowed I were a dead man."

"I thought the bounty hunters got you. I was scared you were dead," Brody said.

"Prolly would have if it weren't for this." Ames pulled a gold eagle out of his pocket.

"What?"

Tossing the gold piece into the air, Ames caught it and put the coin back in his pocket. "The last one I got. We ain't spent it, and it done been bringing us a whole passel of good luck."

Laughing, Brody said, "So you only have one double eagle left, and you think that's good luck?"

Ames sat on what was left of the porch steps. "That crazy wildman didn't kill us. Got me a grandbaby on the way."

Brody nodded. "You might be right. We did get Joseph and Todd back together."

"Got some good old crops coming up."

"Neither one of us are wanted by the law anymore."

"You're back with your folks."

"Everything did work out good, didn't it?" Brody asked.

Ames paused and looked toward the woods. "Them mountains ain't stopped calling, though."

"You miss being up on the Devil's Backbone?"

A grimace came across Ames's face as if what he was about to say caused him great pain. "I just ain't fit for being around folks."

Brody nodded. "I know you miss the mountains. I miss Sarah, but her daddy says I'm bad for her. I guess we can't have things exactly the way we want."

"Many a thing happen on that mountain. Even a place with such a name, God was there. He got a plan." Ames struggled to his feet. "He got a plan for us all."

Brody glanced at Ames's knee. "How's your leg?"

"Fair to middling. Now, tell Ames how come that old Indian were painted red."

Brody looked to see Todd scrubbing hard on Wolf's hands. He chuckled. "That's a long story."

"Look!" Momma called. "Look down the road!"

A line of wagons stretched as far as Brody could see. The first people to arrive were the church ladies. They brought food and warm smiles, but the wagons behind them held people Brody didn't know, hauling supplies, lumber, and tools. The folks of Fort Smith poured onto the property, and tears poured from Momma's eyes.

Calloused hands unloaded timbers and began building a new house right next to the rubble of the old one.

"You don't have to do this," Papa said.

One of the men, a stocky fellow with bushy eyebrows, stopped working for a moment. "It's the least we can do." The other men gave a quick glance and nodded in agreement. Three teenage boys jumped down from yet another wagon and joined in the work.

Papa stood still for a few seconds, just watching all of the bustling activity.

Momma said through her tears, "I can't believe this. I just can't believe all these people came to help."

"There, there, Mrs. Martin," one of the ladies said, giving her a quick hug. "That's what neighbors do. We depend on each other to see us through when times get rough."

Other ladies began to cover the makeshift table with dishes of chicken, potatoes, casseroles, and every sort of thing that Brody's hungry stomach desired. A smaller table was set up nearby with long benches running down the sides of it. Two woven straight-back chairs were placed at either end of the table.

Papa rolled his sleeves up. "Come on, Brody. Let's help with this lumber."

"No, sir," a rather plump lady said.

She took Papa by the arm and motioned Brody and Ames over. "You and Brody get over here, sit down, and eat. There will be no working until you have a good meal in you."

Papa tried to resist, but the woman practically forced him into one of the chairs.

"Come on, Ames," Brody said. "I think there's banana pudding."

"'Banana pudding? I ain't had that in a coon's age."

They wandered over to the food table, and several ladies began loading up plates.

Todd ran up and hugged him around the waist. "Flint, Father says we should be going. He says we need to have a"—Todd spoke carefully—"a 'dee-scush-on.' I think that means we are going to talk about the old Indian. Father says that is his father, and that his father is my grandfather." Todd wrinkled up his forehead, and squinted one eye. "I think he is a grumpy old Indian, but I am going to make him laugh anyway."

Looking toward the well, Brody saw Joseph and Wolf. Joseph smiled and waved. Wolf was wearing his usual frown. Brody grinned. "I bet Wolf is dying to laugh right now," he said.

Todd whooped and yelled, "I will make him laugh, watch me!" He raced away.

Brody headed toward them, but a rosy-cheeked woman wearing a bonnet said, "Where you going? The food will get cold."

"I'll be right back."

When Brody reached Joseph, he was adjusting the saddle on his horse. "You aren't leaving, are you?" Brody asked.

Joseph turned, shook his hand, and said, "You are a man to be remembered."

"You can't leave," Brody said.

Todd had plucked a weed with a feathery top, and he was using it to run along any bare skin on Wolf that he could reach. Wolf twitched.

Joseph said, "We will visit you in the future."

"I want you to stay and eat. There's enough food for everybody."

Todd was standing on tiptoes trying to make the weed reach Wolf's ear. "Tickle, tickle," he whispered loudly. Wolf's right eye twitched, and he smacked at his ear. Todd burst out in giggles. One corner of Wolf's mouth turned up.

Joseph glanced at the men who were carrying lumber and then to the ladies fretting with the dishes of food. "These people do not wish to have Indians at their table."

"Not a one of them has said any such thing," Brody protested. "I want all of you to eat with us. My folks care very much for Todd, and it will hurt Momma's heart if you leave now."

Wolf was watching him. His face seemed different, and Brody finally figured it out. There were fewer stern lines marring it. It occurred to him that the old Indian's scowl was gone.

Todd gave up pestering Wolf and grabbed Brody and Joseph's hands. He started swinging them back and forth. "Can we stay and eat? Can we, Father, can we?" he wheedled.

Joseph rolled his eyes to the sky and sighed.

Todd smiled. "Yes! Come on, Brody, let's get us some food!"

Brody allowed the boy to pull him toward the table. He heard Joseph talking to Wolf in Cherokee as they followed along behind. Papa sat at one end of the table with Momma to his right. Ames sat across from her with Mary next to him. The woman with the bonnet and red cheeks led Brody to the other end of the table and pushed him into the seat. "You will be in the place of honor," she declared with a smile. "The head of the table for today."

Joseph settled into the seat at his right. Wolf sat next to Joseph, but Todd ran around so he could be to Brody's left.

He poked Brody's ribs and laughed. "Bet I can eat more than you."

An open two-wheeled carriage appeared on the lane. Papa said, "Why, I do believe that is Doc Slaughter's buggy." He raised an eyebrow and looked at Brody.

Brody sprung to his feet, bumping the table and rattling dishes as he did. "Sarah!" He knew he was grinning ear to ear as he ran to the buggy, and probably looked ridiculous, but it just could not be helped.

Sarah's sweet laughter filled the air, and she jumped down into Brody's arms before her father could get around to help her out. Brody felt his cheeks heat up, but he took his time before reluctantly letting her go. His knew the folks were watching them, and he heard a few chuckles.

Doctor Slaughter approached Brody's father and mother. "I hope we aren't late."

"Not at all," Momma said. "Would you like some food?"

He looked to Brody. "No, ma'am. I believe I've had all the crow I can eat." He smiled, patted Brody on the shoulder, and then went to help the men working on the house.

Wrinkling his eyebrows, Brody looked at Sarah. "What was that supposed to mean?"

"It's his way of saying he is sorry," she said.

Brody swallowed hard. "Oh. Oh? Umm, you mean you can be my girl? Well . . . if you want to be, that is." Brody glanced at his friends and family around the table and blushed even harder. Everyone got busy loading up plates or looking anywhere but at them.

Sarah hugged him and whispered in his ear. "I'm your girl."

Todd suddenly popped up right beside Brody and Sarah and forced his way between them.

"Sit by me, Sarah," Todd crowed.

Everyone burst out into laughter. Sarah grinned good-naturedly and let Todd lead her to the seat next to his.

Papa blessed the meal, and everyone started eating. The food was simply wonderful, the best Brody could remember having in a long, long while.

Wolf and Joseph ate slowly while watching everyone and listening to their conversations. Ames pulled a biscuit apart, steam rising from its middle.

"Papa," Brody said. "What finally got Miller caught?"

Laughing, Papa said, "Well, you did. After you ran off again."

Momma threw her napkin down in mock anger. "That's right, Brody Martin. You better not ever leave like that again."

An uneasy chuckle went around the table.

"I won't," Brody assured her. "I promise."

Papa continued. "When we found out you were gone, we decided . . . ," he looked at Momma and laid a hand over hers, "that is, your Momma decided there was only one thing we could do. We went straight to the courthouse."

Momma picked up her fork and speared a few green beans. "We knew it was risky, but we demanded to speak directly to the judge."

"Judge Parker?"

"Yes. We waited for nearly two hours, but he finally came."

Papa swallowed a mouthful of food. "We told him everything that had happened, and that's when we found out the Millers were already in a bunch of trouble."

Momma took a drink of sweet tea. "Those ledgers and papers you left at the courthouse had crooked land contracts and all sorts of things in there. The judge told us a warrant was out on Billy and not to worry about the Millers anymore."

"The law made sure we had a safe place to stay until Billy was brought in," Papa said. "Then we gave our statements to the commissioner. They found you at the last minute, and you know the rest."

"I can hardly believe it," Brody said.

Everyone ate and talked about the events that had transpired. Stories of Brody's and Ames's experiences were repeated until Momma held up her hands and said she couldn't take any more.

While the church ladies were bringing dessert, Ames placed his hands on the table and stood. "I'd like to say something."

He cleared his throat and studied Brody for a moment.

"This here li'l fella has had more adventure than most folk. Done more for me than any other. I ain't ever seen a braver man. He come up on that mountain and took me for a friend, didn't matter that I were black, didn't matter that I weren't in my right mind." The big man's eyes were shiny with unshed tears. "I just want to thank ye for everything ye done. For taking me as I were. No finer soul have I ever met."

"We love you, Brody. Both of us," Mary said softly.

Ames sat, and Joseph cleared his throat. "At the stables in Fort Smith last year, I saw a troubled boy. I offered to hire him on because I needed help with trapping—and help with this cub." He reached over and chucked Todd under the chin, making him giggle and squirm. "But Brody was no tenderfoot farm boy. He treated my son like his brother, and when evil came, he risked his life to protect him." He looked to Ames. "Both of you did."

Wolf pointed at Brody. "Unalii."

Joseph nodded.

"He said that to me before. You-Gnaw-Lee." Brody interjected. "What does it mean?"

Joseph put a hand on Brody's shoulder. "It means *friend*."

"Good friend," Wolf added.

Brody saw Joseph's eyes grow wide and realized his own eyes must look the same. "You know English?"

"How?" Joseph asked Wolf. "I've tried to teach you, but you would never listen."

Wolf held his hand up, palm out. "Brody feel . . ." He struggled for the right word, "shame. Shame for white people." He tapped his forehead. "Wolf feel shame. He blame *all* white people." Wolf tried to speak more but gave up his search for the correct words and spoke in his language instead.

He ran his finger along his arm as he talked.

Joseph interpreted. "Our skin is red."

Wolf pointed to Ames.

"His skin is black," Joseph said.

Wolf's finger shifted to others at the table.

"Their skin is white."

Wolf placed his wrinkled hand on his chest.

"Our hearts are all the same."

Wolf swallowed hard and spoke softly.

"Brody showed me this," Joseph said.

Brody realized his mouth was hanging open. He closed it. "Joe, could he understand me all along?" He looked to Wolf. "Could you understand me the whole time?"

Wolf pointed at Todd. His voice rose as it filled with emotion and then fell to little more than a whisper.

Joseph remained quiet for a second. "He said he was a boy, not much older than Todd, when he was led along the Trail of Tears. Our people were bitter, and he has hated all white men since . . . until he met you."

Joseph looked to Brody. "It is a great honor that you have given my father this vision, these new eyes to look through." He nudged Wolf. "But Brody did not teach you to speak English. What about your old ways? Your talk of tradition?"

Wolf winked at Todd, and Todd laughed.

The boy's giggles spread to everyone at the table. Brody caught Sarah's gaze over Todd's head. She smiled, sharing his joy. His world was right once more.

Chapter Seventeen

After eating a hearty meal, everyone joined in the work on the house, except Todd and Wolf. It tickled Brody to see Wolf playing games with Todd while Joseph passed boards up to men on the roof. Brody fetched nails, tools, and anything he was sent after.

With a multitude of hands, the home took shape quickly. The frame was up in no time. Some workers formed an assembly line and hauled up materials, as others pounded nails into the overlapping cedar shakes. The roof was soon finished, and everyone turned their attention to the plank siding.

The walls were finished near sunset, just in time as dark clouds moved in. Countless handshakes, back pats, and hugs were exchanged. Papa and Momma thanked everyone many times over, and Brody stood with them and waved as almost all the wagons left, stretching out into a long line.

It was the finest cabin Brody had ever seen. Not because of any fancy crafting—after all, the house was still just a shell waiting to be filled. Cabinets and furniture had to be built or bought, and they would need to add a porch. It was the fact that the people had opened their hearts to his family, to do such a thing as this. Brody felt humbled and blessed.

Sarah walked up and reached for his hand. Her fingers twined around his. "We're leaving before it starts raining. Will I see you tomorrow?"

He grinned as if he had received the best present ever. "I sure hope so."

She tilted her head and said rather pertly, "Good. I'll be watching for you."

He watched her get into her father's wagon and leave. Brody smiled. He had his family back—and he had his girl.

Ames and Mary came over. "We gonna be leaving."

Todd ran a circle around everyone. "Father says we are leaving too." He stopped and grabbed Momma's hand. "I don't want to leave."

Joseph and Wolf walked up to them just as thunder rumbled in the distance.

"Nobody's leaving," Momma said. Ames started to speak, but Momma cut him short. "We have a brand new house, it's getting dark, and a storm's coming. It's too far to travel. Everyone is staying here tonight."

Joseph glanced at Wolf. "We will camp over there." He pointed at the yard.

"Everyone is staying in the house," Momma said with a firm tone. "And that's it."

She led Todd away from the group and up the temporary wooden steps just outside the door. She looked over her shoulder. "Come on."

"You heard her," Papa said.

Joseph laughed.

The house was empty, with no furniture and no interior walls, just a large rectangular room. Momma spread blankets in one corner for Papa and herself. Joseph and Wolf claimed another corner by placing their bedrolls there, and Ames and Mary settled near the doorway.

Rain came and pelted the new roof, but not a drop found its way inside. Todd bounced all around the house, talking constantly. "Let's play chase. Somebody chase me." He ran and flopped on the floor next to Brody. "Let's go get my treasure."

Brody smiled. "What treasure? I don't remember any treasure."

"Yes you do. The box we hid by the tree. It has all my treasures inside."

Scratching his chin as if thinking hard, Brody said, "I don't know. Are you sure it was me?"

"Flint," Todd scolded. "Stop teasing."

"All right," Brody said. "But it's storming outside. We can get it first thing in the morning."

Todd fell back onto a blanket. "Good. I want to play hully gully. Flint?"

"Yes?"

"I don't think I want to call you Flint anymore. Everyone calls you Brody."

"I told you my real name was Brody. Remember?"

"I remember," Todd said. He glanced toward his father and then whispered, "You told a fib."

"I did, and I shouldn't have."

Todd's whisper continued, "Pop says we shouldn't tell fibs."

"I won't tell any more lies," Brody said.

"So, I can call you Brody?"

"You call me whatever you want."

There was a short pause before Todd giggled. "Maybe I will call you Knot-head."

Everyone laughed, and Todd played it up for his audience. "Or maybe Musket Mouth!"

"Musket Mouth?" Brody said. "What does that even mean?"

Todd paused. "How about . . . Chicken Donkey?" He burst with laughter, which quickly spread around the room.

At daybreak the next morning Brody was awakened by a constant tapping on his forehead. Todd's face was inches from his. "My treasure?"

Swatting Todd's hand away, Brody rubbed his eyes. "I'm getting up. Fetch me a drink of water, and we will go get it."

Todd rushed off.

Momma and Mary were preparing some of the leftover food for breakfast. Wolf and Joseph were talking in the corner with

Papa. Brody looked outside and saw Ames standing in the yard, staring at hills in the distance.

"I'm going out to talk to Ames."

Mary came over. Her voice was soft and hesitant. "He's been out there awhile. He just don't rest much anymore."

Brody went out and leaned against the front wall of the house. "Did you sleep well?"

Ames looked over his shoulder and smiled. "I been out here for some fresh air."

It was clear to Brody that there was more on Ames's mind than getting fresh air. "Something bothering you?"

Turning around and facing him, Ames bent and picked up a piece of wood scrap. He didn't answer with words, but his face answered the question.

"What is it?"

Ames tilted his head and tossed the wood. "Thought I'd feel different, but I don't. Guess I just feeling a li'l lost."

"Why you feeling lost? Our lives can get back to normal now."

"Reckon I'm a long way from normal." Ames smiled.

Brody chuckled. After the humor had died away, he said, "I felt lost one time, remember? But you found me and made sure I got home. You'll be fine."

"What we gonna do now?" Ames asked.

"Keep on being friends. We're going to just keep on being friends."

Ames nodded. "Yes, sir. We surely will."

Todd opened the door.

"You want to go with us?" Brody asked Ames.

"Where to?"

Todd ran out of the house. "We are going to find my treasure box."

Ames grinned at the boy, then looked back toward the foggy hills on the horizon. "I believe I'll look out yonder a while longer. We gonna have to get going anyways."

"You could stay a few more days," Brody said.

Mary came out. "We have to get back. Anna is probably wondering where we are. Amos, can you fetch the wagon that man said we could borrow?"

Ames nodded, but his gaze stayed with the rolling landscape.

Leaning over to Brody, Mary whispered, "Could you go with him? It's just across the river."

Brody sensed the worry Mary was carrying. She was watching Ames. "I'll go with him," he whispered.

Ames reached for Brody's shoulder and pulled him closer. Patting him on the back, he said, "You gonna be here when I gets back?"

Brody nodded. "I think I'm going to give you some company to pick the wagon up."

Todd yanked on Brody's shirtsleeve.

"That sounds fine," Mary said brightly. "Just fine."

Ames said, "Let's get a-going then."

Todd jumped up and down, pulling on Brody's arm. "No, no. We got to find my treasure. Hurry, 'cause Father said we have to leave this morning."

Brody looked to Mary and then Ames. "It won't take but a minute. I'll find his box and then catch up with you."

"We will have some food ready by the time you get back with the wagon," Mary said. She turned back to Brody. "Don't be too long or we might eat it all."

Brody smiled. He looked down at Todd. "We got to hurry."

The boy pulled his hair straight up in frustration and made a face. "That is what I have been saying. Now let's hurry."

Ames waved as he walked toward his mule.

"I'll be right along behind you, Ames," Brody said.

They headed down into the clearing behind the house, with Brody leading the way. "You have to help me look."

Todd left him to run ahead, shouting, "I will! I will find it first!"

Brody went to the southeast corner of the property where

the woods started. "Come here," he called to Todd. "We have to find a funny shaped tree."

Todd ran to his side. His shoes were covered in mud. "Where?"

"Somewhere close," Brody said. "It's two young oaks that have grown around a third tree."

"They grew around it?"

Brody walked and motioned for Todd to follow. "They grew around the smaller tree, and it looks like the little oaks are holding hands on the other side."

"That's where my treasure is?" Todd asked. He giggled. "That's funny."

"It's not there," Brody explained. "That was my marker."

"Here it is!" Todd yelled, pointing at the odd set of trees Brody had described. "Right here!"

"Now we can find it," Brody said. "Step it off with me."

"Which way?" Todd asked.

"Southwest," Brody said. "Forty steps. Are you ready?"

"Yes, sir."

Brody put his back to the tree and faced southwest. "Count my steps for me."

Todd counted as Brody stepped. But at thirty-two strides, they came to a stop. The rainwater had collected in a small rocky drainage that crossed the back of their land.

"It's not deep," Todd said. "We can keep going." He moved forward.

Brody stopped him. "It was dry when I hid it. I put rocks around it, but all that water . . ."

Somebody whistled and whooped from the house.

Brody turned around. "They're calling for us. We can get it when you come back to visit. The water will drain off quickly, and it should be dry in a matter of days. We can find it easy next time you come."

Todd had started to frown, but then his face lit up. "You mean I am coming back? To see you and Mawmee? Yippee!"

Brody laughed.

Todd poked Brody in the middle of his stomach. "It's okay. I'm too grown up for that stuff anyway."

"What about the things your father gave you?"

"I've got Father back. We can get those things later, like you said."

Back at the house, they found Wolf and Joseph, packed and ready. Wolf was already up on his horse, silently meditating on the skyline.

"I don't want to go yet," Todd said.

Momma hugged Todd. "Your father has agreed to let you stay with us from time to time."

Todd's mouth dropped open for a second, then he snapped it shut. "Is it true?"

Joseph helped Todd up and got him settled on the horse. "You will be back before you know it." He turned to Brody and shook his hand. "We will return soon. Stay safe."

"I will," Brody said.

Wolf winked at Brody, then his wrinkled old face moved every so slightly, forming a tiny smile. Brody was almost too dumbfounded to smile back. Almost.

Joseph climbed onto his horse. "Todd will spend much time here. I will see to it. Family is important."

Brody held his hand up. "If you can wait just a minute, I can ride with you to town. I've got to catch up with Ames."

"Yes!" Todd shouted.

Brody laughed and ran to get Buck. After he saddled the horse and rode back around front, he saw Papa, Momma, and Mary waving goodbye to Wolf and Joseph.

"I'll be back in a little while," Brody said as he rode by.

"Be ready for some work," Papa said. "We have to get this house finished up."

"Yes, sir."

"We need to build some walls, unless you enjoy us all sleeping in the same room."

Momma laughed and put her arm around Papa's waist. Papa pulled her close.

"Let's please build some walls," Brody said with a smile.

They made a small group as they rode toward Fort Smith, talking along the way. Wolf spoke very little. He had his hands full with Todd sitting behind the saddle, sometimes hanging on, sometimes tickling Wolf's ear with a weed. Wolf would slap the side of his head and reach behind to grab at the weed, to Todd's delight.

Joseph talked of his plans for the next trapping season, and Todd butted in to tell how he and Brody couldn't find his treasure box.

As they reached town, Joseph shushed Todd. "Brody, we must stop at the store for a few supplies. Would you join us?"

Brody shook his head. "I've got to head toward the ferry and catch up with Ames. I told him I would."

Joseph offered his hand. "We will see each other again."

Shaking with this man Brody had come to love, he could only say, "Soon."

He rode away, waving at Todd and Wolf. Todd waved back wildly. Wolf nodded and smiled slightly. Kicking Buck's sides, Brody trotted through the streets.

A dark horse pulling a black open carriage dashed quickly out of a side lane, swinging wide and nearly tipping the whole thing over. A girl was pulling frantically on the leads, trying to straighten out the buggy.

"Sarah!" Brody shouted in surprise.

She yanked back on the reins, causing the horse to stiffen its legs and dig its hooves into the muddy street. They came to an abrupt stop. "Brody! I am so glad I found you."

"What is it?"

"I was headed to your place!"

Brody felt his heart sink. "What's wrong, what has happened?"

Sarah pointed toward the jail. "Nothing is wrong, really, but it is important. Billy Miller is dead."

Chapter Eighteen

Brody sputtered. "D-d-dead? How?"

"Last night," Sarah said. "It happened last night."

"Hang on, Sarah." Brody climbed off Buck's back and tied his reins to the rear of her buggy. He pulled himself into the seat next to her and gestured toward the river. "Tell me about it on the way to the ferry. We need to catch up with Ames and tell him."

She turned the buggy around in the street and then slapped the leathers against the horse. The bay startled, then leaned into the harness, trotting quickly. As soon as they cleared the main street, Sarah popped the reins and they moved off at a fast gallop.

Brody held tight as the carriage bounced on the rutted road. "What happened?"

"A mob of people forced their way in. Daddy said he heard most of them were wearing masks. They overpowered the jailers and took Billy."

"What did they do to him?"

"They lynched him."

"You mean they strung him up?"

"That is right. Come daylight, he was swinging in a tree on his own property."

A guilty sort of relief came over him, but even though the man deserved death, the manner in which it came seemed wrong. "I guess that's the end of it then."

She said, "Well, it certainly is the end of Billy Miller."

They were making good time, and Brody thought they should see Ames on his mule soon. Sarah turned the buggy toward the river.

"It's over," Brody said. "I don't have to go to court or worry about him getting out." He paused. "I hate he had to die. I didn't want anybody to die."

"I know it, Brody, but he tried to kill you." Her voice hardened. "I think he deserved what he got."

"Remind me to never get on your bad side, Sarah Slaughter."

They arrived at the corral by the ferry, but the operator was nowhere to be seen. The door of the shack by the river's edge stood open as if someone had left in a hurry. A big mule wandered across the road in front of them, nibbling at the grass.

"That's Ames's mule." Prickles ran along Brody's skin. Ahead, fifty steps from the rolling water, lay a man's body.

"Ames!" A mixture of anger and fear raged in Brody's core. Without thinking, he jumped from the moving buggy, his feet thumping against the ground.

"Be careful," Sarah called after him.

Brody scrambled toward the fallen man, off-balance, nearly falling. A red spot of blood had formed on the right side of Ames's chest, near his armpit. Brody leaned close and placed a hand behind his neck. "Ames! Who shot you?"

The black man was pale, and his head lolled to the side as Brody tried to raise him. "Ames!"

Sarah arrived at his side. "Oh, Brody, he looks awful."

The left side of his forehead was swollen with a bulbous knot, and bloody matter had clotted the center of the bullet hole in his chest.

"Frank did this," Brody said. "I just know it. Ames needs help, Sarah."

Sarah held Ames's wrist for a moment. "I . . . It's . . ." She let go of his arm, her eyes bright with tears. "I'll get my father."

"Hurry, Sarah, get help as fast as you can."

She dashed to the back of the buggy and yanked Buck's reins free. She came around and leaped onto the seat, gathering the leads up and popping them against the horse's back. "Get on up, Aster! Heeya, get up!" Buck took a few steps after the buggy before stopping to watch it race back up the road.

Brody watched Ames for signs of life. His chest did not rise or fall, and the blood crept down the fabric of his shirt. "No, Ames!" Brody cried in anguish. "You can't be dead."

Unstoppable tears spilled from Brody's eyes. He slumped over onto Ames and sobbed.

Ames coughed.

Jolting as if lightning had struck him, Brody jerked back onto his knees, holding his breath. Ames's eyes fluttered open.

Brody pulled his shirt out of his pants and tore off part of the tail. He pressed it over the wound that was bubbling with each slight breath Ames took. "I thought you were dead."

Ames looked at him with hazy eyes and fumbled to put his hand over Brody's. Large tears trailed down the side of the man's face. "I were running so fast," he whispered.

Brody shook his head. "You weren't running."

"I were running down a grassy hill, Brody." Ames cleared his throat and his voice grew a little stronger. "My leg weren't hurting no more, and they were a lake so smooth, so still and clear."

His pupils shrank to pinpoints, and he closed his eyes. "Seen some folk having a picnic. They had 'em a mighty fine spread of food."

Brody leaned close and fought to keep from crying. "You're not making any sense. Hush, now, and save your strength. Did Frank do this?"

Ames opened his eyes and more tears came. "Them folks, Brody. Them folks was my ma and pa."

"You're confused again, Ames. It's gonna be okay. Sarah's gone for help. Who shot you?"

Ames squeezed Brody's hand. "I'm gonna go back to that place someday."

"Not today," Brody retorted. "I keep losing you, and you keep coming back. One of these days you won't come back at all, but today is not that day, you understand me?"

Brody felt his chest tighten when Ames closed his eyes again. "Ames, open your eyes! Doctor Slaughter is on his way."

Ames opened his mouth to say something but stopped. His eyes snapped open and became clear and focused. "Frank," he whispered harshly. "He shot me."

"I knew it! Where is he?"

The sandy dirt next to them exploded, and a gunshot roared from nearby. "Get over here!" Someone shouted.

There was Frank, pointing a pistol at him as he stood on the ferry platform. He held the gun tight and kept it pointed at Brody. "He's as good as dead and you are too, unless you get over here. Now!"

Brody looked down at Ames. His face was so pale, but his eyes were burning fiercely. "Run, Brody. Run off and hide."

Brody moved his hand from the soaked fabric around the wound and placed Ames's hand over it. Ames groaned and closed his eyes again.

Brody couldn't bring himself to abandon his friend, not while he was hurt. A cold anger coursed through his body, steeling his nerves and filling him with purpose. Slowly, he stood up and stepped toward the ferry. "Put the gun down. Nobody has to get killed."

Frank's cheeks looked like he had been slapped hard, each with a wide blotch of red, just like his hair. His face was contorted with anger. The extra wrinkles made him look much older. "You killed my Pa!" he shouted. "You dirty little pie-eating farm boy. You ruined my life."

Brody kept a steady pace toward the ferry, until he reached the small shack. He stopped. "You ruined your own life. I didn't kill Billy. He did that to himself."

Glancing over, he noticed one of the ferrymen lying still in the doorway, blood puddled around his head. Turning back to face Frank, Brody said, "We don't have to fight anymore. We can end all of this."

"Get over here, now!" Frank yelled.

"What do you want?" Brody moved closer but stopped a few steps from the river. "I'll come on the ferry as soon as Ames gets some help."

Frank redirected the gun away from Brody and toward Ames. "Come on right now, or he won't be needing any help."

Moving forward slowly, Brody did his best to come up with a plan.

Unarmed. His gun was lost at the Devil's Den. He had given his knife to Wolf.

Once again, he was helpless when he needed a weapon the most. Brody squeezed his hands into hard fists, so tightly that his knuckles popped. He wasn't completely helpless. If he could get close enough to Frank, he would fight for all he was worth.

Frank came to the edge of the ferry and grabbed Brody by the shirt. Yanking hard, he pulled him onto the ferry and then slung him sideways.

Brody lost his balance and fell. He landed facedown with his head and shoulders hanging over the side, just above the swirling water. Frank put a foot on his back, cocked the pistol, and shoved the barrel against the back of his neck.

Brody froze. "Wait! There's no need for this."

"Hush," Frank ordered.

Brody looked for anything that could help him get out of this situation. He saw some thick ferry rope, a pair of boots, and somebody's lunch pail. None of that could save him.

Frank reached into his pocket, brought out a pair of hand-cuffs, and dropped them next to Brody. "Put them on." Frank kicked him in the side.

Brody gasped at the shooting pain. "Please, Frank, let it go. You don't want to hang for our murders."

Frank's jaw clamped tight, causing the muscles to stand out on the side of his face. A vein bulged on his neck. "You are pushing me too far. Get those cuffs on or I'll kill you right here."

Brody slowly rolled to his side. He placed one of the cuffs around his left wrist and pulled the key cylinder up until it clicked. He hesitated before slowly securing the second cuff on his other hand. "Now what?"

"Sit down over there." He gave a sour chuckle and gestured toward the far bank. "We are going to cross the river, and then I'm cutting the ferry loose. You and I are going for a walk, and I can guarantee you will not enjoy what happens next, but I promise *we* certainly will."

Glancing across the water, Brody recognized Carl and Lester, the two bounty hunters who had hounded him from Ames's farm to the Devil's Den. They were still black and blue from the beating Eugene had given them. Brody knew they would be overjoyed at a chance to get even with him.

Letting out a long sigh, Brody said, "Frank, I . . ."

Shots pierced the air. Frank flinched, firing his pistol by mistake. The bullet splintered the wood next to Brody's waist.

Looking in the direction of the shots, Brody saw Ames stumbling away from the ferry building with a gun. He fired over and over, and Frank blasted back with his six-shooter. Brody crawled for cover behind the wooden bench on the ferry.

Frank kicked at Brody but missed. He fired at Ames again, but Ames charged ahead with no regard for the flying lead. By the time he reached the platform, Ames was leaning forward, his upper body almost even to the ground.

They collided like two raging bulls. Empty pistols rattled across the wood floor, a hat tumbled into the river, and dirt flew from Ames's muddy boots. The two men tumbled into a flailing heap, rolling and punching.

"Stop!" Brody shouted. He pulled hard against his restraints but couldn't free his hands. A loud splash came from the far end of the ferry, and Brody looked in time to see the two men disappearing into the swollen river.

Brody grabbed the bench to pull himself up and rushed to the spot where they went in. He saw Ames spitting water and reaching for the ferry.

Going to his knees, he grabbed one of Ames's hands with both of his and pulled. "I got you." The force of the current surprised him, and it took all his might to get Ames closer.

Just as he began to make progress, Frank exploded out of the water, grabbing Ames around the neck in a headlock. The weight of two bodies was too much for Brody. His wet grip gave way until his fingertips hooked Ames's. Even though Brody squeezed as hard as he could, their fingers slipped apart. He made a wild grab, desperately reaching for Ames, but it was too late.

They locked eyes for a brief moment, and then Ames twisted around and punched Frank.

"Ames!" Brody jumped to his feet and ran to the very corner of the ferry.

He could see the two men, still fighting, as they were swept downriver. Ames tried to push Frank under, but Frank had a death grip on him and they both disappeared. Brody started to jump in but stopped, realizing he couldn't swim with his hands cuffed.

"Ames!"

Ames popped back to the surface with Frank still clutching his shirt. They were spitting, coughing, struggling . . . and the river was taking them away.

Brody noticed a flurry of movement on the far bank. He had forgotten about Lester and Carl. The bounty hunters sat astride their horses, headed away from the river at a gallop. He sprinted off the ferry and onto the bank. As he turned to run along the river's edge, he saw Sarah arriving with her father.

Pointing with his bound hands, Brody shouted, "Frank and Ames fell in! They are in the water!"

When he looked back, Ames and Frank had disappeared around a bend. Brody ran harder, so hard that he lost control and crashed into some brush. Fighting to catch his breath, he got back to his feet and rushed up the side of a rise.

At the top, trees mostly blocked his view of the river. With eager eyes, he watched the sections of water between the trees, hoping to see Ames. He started down the other side of the hill, but Sarah grabbed his arm. "Wait, Brody, help is coming. I told them you thought Frank did it."

Two deputies on horseback brushed past them and slid to a stop. "Was it Frank?" one of them asked.

"Yes," Brody said. "Frank shot Ames. They are both in the river!"

Pulling with all his strength against the cuffs, Brody slid his hand out, tearing the skin off the outside of his thumb. "Ames. Get Ames! He's hurt bad." The deputies spun their horses and pushed through the thick brush.

Brody kept moving forward, leaving a bloody trail, with Sarah right behind him. They lost sight of the deputies' horses as they approached the river's edge.

When Brody reached the water again, he was exhausted. Fighting the tangle of saplings and weeds had sapped him of all strength. The high water had left no clear bank to walk on, making each step a challenge.

"Ames! Where are you?" he called.

"What happened?" Sarah asked from behind him.

Brody's mind seemed to be scrambled. He shook his head. "I think Ames got a gun off the dead ferryman."

"But Ames was hurt."

"I don't know how he did it, but he came down on Frank like an avalanche. They fell in the river, fighting the whole way."

"We'll find him, Brody. We are going to find him."

Brody stepped over a log and stared across the muddy water. "He was hurt bad, Sarah. He can't swim long."

"The deputies will get him out. They have ropes on their saddles."

"Remember his bad leg his master broke when he was young?"

"But he's tough," Sarah pointed out.

Brody nodded. "Toughest man I know."

They walked for another half hour without finding any sign of Ames. Brody trudged onward with blood dripping from the thumb on his left hand and the cuffs swinging from his right wrist. Sarah stayed right behind him but kept quiet.

One of the deputies rode up with Buck trailing behind. Brody's horse whinnied at him as the deputy dropped his reins. "Y'all come on. We found him." The man turned his horse and rode back toward the ferry.

"You found Ames?" Brody shouted after him, but he was already out of sight. "They found Ames!" Brody said to Sarah. He climbed on Buck and helped Sarah up. She wrapped her arms around him and held on while they twisted left and right, weaving through the brush by the river.

As they came to the ferry, Brody saw that a crowd had gathered. The sheriff and his deputies were trying to keep people back. A crying woman was kneeling next to the dead ferryman.

Brody helped Sarah down, and then slid out of the saddle. "Where is he?"

The deputy pointed to a blanket covering a body. Brody's knees nearly buckled. He couldn't blink. He couldn't breathe.

Chapter Nineteen

"He drowned," the lawman said.

Brody felt as if he could throw up. "Ames. No. Please no."

"It's not Ames," the man said. "It's Frank. We haven't found Ames yet."

Sarah took Brody by the arm. Her eyes were wide.

"That's Frank?" he asked, weak with relief.

The deputy nodded. "I have some questions for you."

Brody stared at the blanket, the big lump under the blanket, the worthless excuse for a human. He pulled free from Sarah's grip and took four quick strides. He reared back to deliver the hardest kick he could muster, but Sarah yanked his arm, making him miss.

He locked gazes with her and realized how angry he must look. "He deserves it, Sarah. I just wish he was alive so he could feel me kicking him."

Shaking her head, she said, "I know you are hurting, Brody, but it still does not make it right."

"Tell me what happened," the lawman said.

Brody stared at the blanket. He still wanted to kick Frank. "I need to go look for Ames. Can we do this later?"

The deputy's voice remained flat and teetered on uncaring. "What happened?"

Speaking quickly, Brody said, "I was to catch up with Ames. We found him over there on the ground. He had been knocked in the head and shot. There was a dead man by the building, and Frank had a gun. He made me put these on." Brody held his arm up and let the cuffs dangle.

The lawman pulled a key from his pocket, reached out, and removed the handcuffs. "What else?"

"Somehow, Ames got up and came at Frank. They went into the water and fought all the way downstream."

"Anything else?"

"There were two bounty hunters across the river but they hightailed it. Now, can I go look for Ames?"

"Bounty hunters?"

"They caught me up north. They were going to take me to Billy."

"Know their names?"

"Just their first names. They called each other Lester and Carl. Hey, I really need to go."

"We have people looking," the man said. "You need to go on home."

Doctor Slaughter walked to the ferry, leading Mary to a wooden bench. She was slouched over and crying.

"Oh, no," Brody said. "Sarah, can you tell her what happened?"

Sarah joined them, leaving Brody with the lawman.

Momma seemed to appear out of thin air. "Oh, Brody, are you hurt?" Turning him to face her, she looked him over. "You are bleeding!" Papa walked up behind her.

"I'm fine, Momma. Stop fussing, please."

Taking his hand, she said, "Son, you are dripping blood everywhere." She looked pointedly at the deputy. "Can you at least get him a bandage? See if Doc has a clean one."

The lawman started to protest. Momma cut in curtly, "Now, sir." The man shut his mouth and left, presumably to find a bandage.

She noticed the blanket. "Who's that?"

"Frank," Brody said. "Ames is missing. He's hurt bad."

Papa put a hand on Momma's shoulder and pointed in Mary's direction. "Oh, poor Mary," she said. She turned back to Brody. "Are you sure you are all right?"

Brody nodded.

"Get that deputy to bandage that tight, you hear?"

Brody nodded again, but Momma was already making her way to Mary. He turned to his father. "Thank you for that."

"It is all right, son. Brody, I hate to hear that Ames is hurt and missing."

"I have to find him!"

The lawman reappeared next to them, a bandage dangling in his hand. "Mister Martin, you need to take your son home."

"I'm not going home," Brody said, taking the white length of cloth and wrapping it around his hand and thumb.

"Either you go home, or I take you to jail."

"To jail?" Papa asked. "Did he do something wrong?"

"You can't be wandering out there with those other men around. It's not safe."

"What men?" Papa asked.

"Your boy said there were bounty hunters with Frank."

"But they left. I told you I saw them riding away."

"It's not safe," the deputy repeated. "I'll do whatever I need to keep you safe, or I'll have to answer to Bass. For some God-forsaken reason he has taken a liking to you."

Brody studied the man's face, hoping for a wink or some sign that the warning was just sort of an official thing he was required to say.

The lawman's expression remained stern. "I mean it. Go home and we will give you news just as soon as we can. We will find Andrew soon."

Tilting his head back, Brody fought to keep his composure. "His name is Amos. I'm going to look for him right now, and you can just take me to jail if you have to."

"You need to take your boy home, Mister Martin, while we keep searching." The man's voice rose. "Everyone needs to clear out!" He whistled and waved one of the marshals over. "We need

to get everyone out of here. He says there were other men helping Frank."

The message spread, and the crowd started to disperse.
Momma showed back up with Mary in tow. "They are making
everybody leave."

"Sarah!" Brody shouted.

"Here I am," she said, coming around the ferry shack.

"Can you and your father make sure Momma and Mary get
home?"

"We will," she said. "You are going back, aren't you?"

"I have to, Sarah."

She reached out and squeezed Brody's good hand. "Be careful, then."

His gaze lingered on her for a moment, before he turned
back to Papa. "Let's go."

They doubled up on Buck, snuck into the woods, and headed
downstream. Brody and Papa searched the ground and water's
edge for any clues.

They had only searched for a short time when they heard
a horse coming through the brush. The same deputy appeared
who had questioned him earlier. "I told you to go home."

"I can't," Brody said. "I'm not leaving Ames out here!"

"Then you and your father are going to jail."

Papa protested. "Can't you just let us look a little longer? The
missing man is very close to my son."

The lawman got off his horse and held a pair of cuffs out.
"Hold your hands out," he said to Brody's father.

Brody opened the door on the family's new cabin. Papa closed
the door behind them, and Brody saw that someone had set up
a makeshift table and brought in two benches. It was the only
furniture yet in the house.

"Did you find him?" Mary must have known the answer

from Brody's solemn face because she broke down and cried on Momma's shoulder.

"The law ran us out," Papa said.

Brody stepped closer to Mary. "We are going back in just a little while. One of the deputies followed us home, but he will leave soon."

"Do what they tell you," Mary said. She sniffed and wiped her face with the towel Momma offered. "You can't do Ames any good if you're locked up."

After consoling Mary, Momma unpacked some food. Everyone sat silently, picking at their plates, not eating, just breathing and letting the events of the day sink in. Rolling thunder in the distance shook Brody from his trance.

"I hope it goes around us. Another storm is the last thing we need."

But the storm came and brought cracks of lightning with it. Thunder boomed. Mary seemed helpless with grief. Momma rubbed her back as she watched Brody.

Wind rattled the door, and rain pelted the ground outside. Papa whittled on a piece of wood. They all had to be thinking the same thing.

Ames could be out there in the storm, floating down the river, lying on the bank, or trying to crawl through the brush. He could be dying or dead. Either way, he shouldn't be alone.

Brody stood. "That's it! I can't stand another minute of this!"

Someone knocked on the door, hard and fast. Papa jumped up to open it, and there stood one of the marshals wearing a long raincoat and big hat. The sound of the rain blocked their exchange from Brody's ears.

Papa closed the door and faced the table. "They have called the search off because of the storm."

Mary groaned. Momma spoke softly to her, but Brody did not listen.

"I'm going out," he said.

His father stayed in front of the door. "You need to wait until tomorrow. It will be dark soon with all the clouds."

"Joseph could help us," Brody said.

Papa opened the door, letting the sound and mist from the rain find its way in. "They left town. I'm sure they don't even know this has happened."

He motioned for Brody. "Grab that piece of canvas to keep your head dry and come to the barn. The horses need tending."

Rain pounded them as they ran to the lean-to barn. Once under the roof, Papa spoke up. "It's not looking good for Ames. There is no other way to say it."

Upon hearing the words he feared, Brody fought the urge to cover his ears. "Papa, please don't think I'm disrespecting you."

"What do you mean?" Papa asked.

"I'm going to look for him. There's still light left for a few hours."

"In the middle of this storm?" Papa shook his head.

"He would do it for me." Brody's voice rose a little louder than he intended. "I have to. If they put me in jail, so be it."

A long pause followed while the storm raged around them. "I don't have any raincoats."

Brody shook his head. "It does not matter. Papa, I have to go."

"You are not going alone."

Brody pulled his slicker out of Buck's saddlebag. "And you are not leaving the women here alone, not with everything that has happened."

"Then we will wait until tomorrow," Papa said.

Brody flung the slicker on and grabbed a saddle blanket. "I have to do this. He would have looked for me. . . ." Brody gritted his teeth and forced the words out. "Or my body."

"Don't do this to me." Papa shook his head. "Don't put me in this spot."

Brody turned and reached for the saddle. He quickly cinched

the girth tight around Buck's belly until the horse grunted. He picked up the hackamore bridle, slipped it up over Buck's nose, and fastened it behind his ears.

His father watched him mount up and walk out into the rain. Brody expected him to come out and try to stop him, but he didn't. Papa stood and watched, surely trying to figure out a solution.

As he left the farm, lightning streaked long jagged fingers across the sky above. When Brody reached Fort Smith, it seemed to be a ghost town. Most businesses had shut down early because of the storm. The empty streets were a muddy mush with water flowing through some of them.

He arrived at the river and found it had risen again. The ferry had been grounded to keep it from being swept away. Pausing, he took in the sight of the swollen water, trying to keep the scene from setting his spirits back even more.

Leaving the road, he cut through the brush, taking his time and trying to make sure Buck didn't slide on the soaked ground. He avoided steep terrain and attempted to yell above the noise from the storm.

"Ames!"

Over and over, he shouted. Thunder drowned him out occasionally but he kept trying, looking, and praying. He made circles and cut back often, doing his best to cover all of the ground he could. There was no hope of finding tracks. The rain had washed away any signs. Even the prints of the deputies were gone.

Water seeped into his clothes, tiny drops tickling his skin, finding all of his dry spots. He jumped down and led Buck along the river. His father's words came back and haunted him. He did not want them to be true. It didn't look good for Ames, but still, he could not give up.

An hour later, it was raining harder than ever. So much water ran down from his hair that Brody had trouble keeping it out of his eyes. He rubbed them, swiped at them, and finally draped

Buck's reins across the horse's neck, pulling the slicker up and over his head like a tent. Peeking out, he walked and continued shouting for Ames while Buck followed behind.

The storm grew, the winds so stiff they caused him to lose balance. Leaning into the gust, he pushed forward. A sharp crack sounded close by. Brody looked in time to see a dead tree falling, taking younger trees down in its path. Minutes later, he broke out of the woods and came to a long patch of cleared land. Looking at the large buildings along the river, he wondered if Ames could have sought refuge there.

Brody started for the first building but stopped dead. The fading light was still enough for him to see something moving in the far distance. His heart hammered, pounding with hope. As the figure approached, Brody realized it was someone on a horse. A second rider came down the hill, joined with the first, and then they headed his direction.

His initial instinct was to run for fear of it being the two bounty hunters, but Brody stood his ground. As the riders closed in, he recognized his father and the second man as Doc Slaughter. Papa rode close and got down, but Doctor Slaughter stayed on his horse.

"We have covered this side of the river for two miles back," Papa said.

Those were the last words Brody had expected to hear. "Where are Momma and Mary?"

"They are at the doctor's home with Sarah."

Brody hugged his father. The gesture triggered a flood of emotions, and he fought to keep from falling apart.

Doctor Slaughter rode by and said, "I'm going to look down in this low spot over here."

When he was gone, Papa held Brody by the shoulders and looked him in the eye. "Ames is not on this side, son."

Brody turned to face the river. It was rolling, tumbling, and wide.

"It's getting dark," Papa said. "We have done all we can."

Cupping his hands around his mouth, Brody desperately yelled across the water. "Ames!" He moved down a little farther before calling again.

His father walked by his side.

"I can't leave yet," Brody insisted.

"We have to," Papa said. "We can't stay out in this all night."

He faced his father and watched water trailing in rivulets off the brim of his hat. Brody remembered how Ames looked when he was lying near the ferry, knocking on death's door. "He could still be alive," he said.

"I know," Papa replied.

"He really could," Brody said as he looked across the river again. "Ames!" Lightning flashed, and the image of Ames flickered in his mind. The gunshot wound was bleeding, and the knot on his head looked horrible. Brody glanced to his father. "You are wrong! He could be alive."

"I didn't say he was dead."

"He's tough," Brody said. "Tough as leather . . ."

His fight against the denial gave way, and he went to his knees, sucking in great gulps of air.

His father knelt next to him and put a hand on his shoulder. Brody shook it off.

"You're wrong! Slavery didn't kill him. The war didn't kill him. And that bear couldn't, it could not kill him!"

"Brody," Papa said, just loud enough to be heard over the pelting rain.

"You're wrong." He shouted through his tears. "You're wrong, Papa." Thunder cracked overhead, and the wind whipped up. Brody howled out the agony in his heart. "I didn't get to say goodbye, Ames. I didn't get to say goodbye!"

Chapter Twenty

Papa sat in the mud and pulled Brody to him. Brody huddled against his father, feeling the rain pummeling him. He remembered being a small child, nestled in his father's lap and wailing over scraped knees as if it were the end of the world. Oh, how he wished he could go back and only have a child's problems.

"I'm sorry, Papa," he whispered miserably, "I'm so sorry I yelled at you."

Brody's father was a man of few words, but what he said was exactly what Brody needed to hear.

"It's all right, son. I understand."

The wind slowly died down, and the rain along with it. Brody felt wrung out and hollow. He sucked in a deep breath and let it out slowly. It was time to quit wallowing in sorrow and find the body of his best friend. It was the most he could do.

"Let's go," he said. "We can make plans for another search when we can cross the river."

The following days were a blur. The bounty hunters were caught by the law, and search parties consisting of sharecroppers and a few marshals covered both sides of the river for miles. Luke had gotten word of what had happened and left Anna in the care of a neighbor before riding down to join them.

Although they did their best, they found no trace of Ames. On the morning of the third day, the effort was halted. After thanking everyone for helping, Brody, his parents, Mary, and Luke gathered with heavy hearts at the new cabin.

Momma did her best to make everyone comfortable. Several more pieces of furniture had appeared while they were out searching, including a rocker and a few more cane-backed chairs. There was food a-plenty, but no one had much of an appetite.

Mary sat her tea glass on the table and looked at Brody with sad eyes. "We done our best."

Brody shook his head. A loud knock saved him from having to answer.

"Come in," Papa called.

The door opened, and there stood Joseph, Wolf, and Todd.

Joseph led the way in, but the boy pushed around him and ran to bear-hug Brody. Brody gathered him up and hugged him back.

Momma stood up to welcome them, and Mary and Luke gave quiet greetings.

Todd pointed at the table.

"What are you eating?" he asked.

Brody chuckled and said, "Are you hungry?"

Todd nodded eagerly.

Wolf leaned against the wall by the door, but Joseph stepped to the table. "We have heard the news and have come to offer any help we can."

"I don't know what else we can do," Mary said.

Brody shook hands with Joseph. The big man's face was full of sympathy and concern. He placed a hand on Brody's arm. "Did you search the north side of the river?"

"We have been miles down both sides." Papa stood and came around to shake with Joseph. He nodded at Wolf, who inclined his head briefly in return.

Mary cleared her throat. "We have found nothing."

Momma swept Todd up in a great hug, slid him into a seat, and proceeded to fill a plate for him, much to his delight.

"Eat," Brody said.

"Yes, everyone eat," Momma said, passing around more plates.

Brody motioned for Wolf to join them. Todd ate and

chattered away, lifting everyone's mood and causing a few grins and chuckles. Momma and Mary talked about Anna and the expected baby.

As they were finishing up the meal, Joseph asked for the story of what happened that day at the ferry. Brody looked askance at Mary, and she nodded. Together they managed to tell the story without breaking down. Joseph softly repeated parts of the story to Wolf.

When they were done, Wolf murmured something in Cherokee.

Joseph said, "My father says, he is grieved these families suffered for the bad choices of evil men. I agree with him."

"Thank you," Brody said quietly.

Mary reached over and patted Luke's hand. He nodded and spoke as he stood up and helped Mary to her feet. "It's time for us to be headed back. Anna is waiting for us to return," Luke said.

"Will you be coming back here soon?" Momma asked.

Mary paused. Her face reminded Brody of a wilted flower, exhausted and tired.

"It's been long enough," she said.

Brody stood. "Long enough? What do you mean, Mary?"

She looked around the room, from one person to the next until she stopped at Brody. "Honey, he was hurt bad."

Brody clenched his hand into fists. "We could look some more."

"It's done, Brody," Mary said. "I wish we could find his body, but it ain't gonna happen. He would be happier to rest out in the woods anyhow."

Her statement made Brody cringe. She had totally given up. The thought of Ames's body had snuck around in Brody's mind, but he had kept it scared away. Now it came bursting forward, the image of him lying alone, washed up by the river.

"I have a grandbaby coming soon," Mary said. Tears streamed out of her eyes as she went to the door.

Luke followed her. "We do need to get back. Ma'am." He nodded at Momma. "Thank you much for opening your home to us."

Mary stopped at the door and reached out for Brody's hand. He placed it in hers, and she pulled him close. "Baby, I know you are gonna miss him so much, but you got to let him go." She pulled back and searched his face. "I will let you know about the funeral as soon as it's arranged."

Funeral? The thought tore Brody apart.

"Bless your heart, Mary," Momma said. She turned to Papa. "Jim, can she have him declared?"

"Given the circumstances, I'm sure she could."

Brody didn't want to hear any more. He went around Mary and stepped outside.

A few days later, Mary sent word for him to meet her at Davis Monument Works in Fort Smith. When he found the building, he went inside and saw Mary waiting for him.

"How have you been?" Brody asked as Mary clasped his hands in greeting.

"I've had better days. Peace gonna find us again. Don't you worry."

A man came through a door in the back. A blast of pounding hammers, grinding and whirring sounds, accompanied him until he slammed the door closed. "Ah, Miz Mary, is this the other party you were waiting to arrive? Are you ready now?"

"Yes, sir," Mary said.

The man reached into a pocket on his apron and pulled out a small ragged notepad and a pencil. He raised the pencil over the pad, poised to take notes. "When was he born?"

"I don't know," Mary answered. "He didn't know either."

"When did he die?"

Mary paused. "Here," she said, handing him a piece of paper. "This is from the court." She brought out another piece of paper. "This is a statement from the sheriff."

The man took the information and looked it over.

"Does this have everything you need?" Mary asked.

"This isn't going to be much of a headstone," the man said. "No birth date, no definite death date, and no last name. It's just going to say *Amos*."

"Martin," Mary said. "Can you put *Martin* under his name?"

Brody turned to Mary in astonishment.

"Like this?" the man interrupted, taking a pencil and drawing an outline on a notebook. He wrote Amos at the top of the headstone sketch and then MARTIN at the bottom.

"Yes," Mary said.

"I'll have it ready next month," he said.

Mary folded the sheets of paper together and followed Brody outside. He paused and stared at the tumbling layer of clouds. A mild breeze twisted its way through the streets, bringing the scent of new blooms in dogwood trees. Mary walked past him and pointed to a bench near the building. "Let's sit down."

Brody was still speechless over adding his family name to the tombstone. Mary continued, "Brody, I know Amos would be proud to have your name on his headstone."

"Is this what you want?" he finally managed to asked.

Mary nodded. "And I know Amos would want the same."

"Thank you for that, but I meant are we giving up on Ames?" Brody asked. "Are we giving up on finding his body? Having an empty grave?"

Mary didn't answer.

Brody sat quietly for a few seconds. "What if he's still alive? He's a tough old goat."

"I would love to find him alive, but you know that is just wishfulness," Mary chided.

"I know," Brody said. "I just don't want to believe it."

"He had a host of problems, Brody. You know that. That old mountain ridge called to him. I think he would have gone back if that knee had not gotten so bad. After being shot and hit on the head, I think he. . . ." She covered her face with both hands and groaned. "He knew he was done. When you said he come rushing at Frank, I think he knew he was dying, and he was set on taking that man with him." Mary dropped her hands and shook her head in sorrow.

Brody thought about everything she had said. Ames didn't hide the fact that he did not fit into his family's life. The memories he carried back with him from the mountain had stayed with him, and sometimes he got them confused with real life.

Frank had hurt him bad. Brody remembered that hole in his chest, spilling blood. Maybe Ames didn't have the will or strength to make it out of the river.

Mary wiped her eyes with a wadded-up handkerchief.

"I shall not wait any longer. Anna will have her baby soon, and that should be a time to rejoice. We have to face the truth and put this behind us," Mary insisted, probably more for Brody's sake than her own.

They sat in silence for a while.

Finally, Mary reached over and patted Brody's leg. "Amos wanted his grandchild to be named after you. Anna and Luke agreed," she said. "If it's a boy, we will name him Brody."

The news brought a mixture of surprise and sadness to him. "I . . . I would be honored."

"Would you ask your mother if she would host a ceremony for the funeral? We live too far from Fort Smith."

"I'm sure she will," Brody said.

"Tell her I don't expect many people. Amos had no friends, except you and yours."

Brody stared across the street. "I can't believe he's gone. I just can't."

She pulled a folded newspaper out of her bag. "Have you read this?"

"What is it?"

"You and Amos made the front page."

Brody unfolded the paper and saw a bold headline announcing that former deputy Billy Miller had been lynched by a mob of angry citizens. The article described some of the charges that had been filed against him and how Brody and Ames had brought forth evidence leading to the charges.

It also explained that the ex-slave, Amos, had been suspected of killing his masters during the war, but it was Billy Miller and his brother who had framed him. The last part of the article dealt with Frank's death and told of Amos being shot and swept away. Brody winced as he read it and stopped before reaching the end.

"That . . . That's hard to read."

"I thought the same," Mary said.

"I can't believe they summed it all up that quick." The thought of Ames's life being wrapped up in a short article bothered him. It wasn't that simple. Why couldn't they write about his life, not his death?

The day came, the dreaded time they would say goodbye to Ames. The windows in the house had been covered in black fabric. An empty wooden casket sat on the table. Just the sight of it gave Brody the creeps.

When Mary came, she was dressed in black from head to toe. Luke helped her inside and then brought Anna to the table. Anna's belly was stretched tight, and she held it protectively with both hands while Luke helped her sit.

Momma stayed busy cooking on the old stove salvaged from the burned cabin while everyone else made awkward conversation. "I don't think we will have enough food," Momma said.

Mary managed a smile. "Don't you worry none, I'm sure there will be plenty. We don't expect very many folks to show up. We just don't know many people."

"Joseph said he would be here," Brody said.

"Doctor Slaughter and Sarah," Papa added.

"Oh, and our preacher is going to speak, if it is okay with you and your family," Momma said.

Mary nodded. "Of course." She turned to face Brody. "Can you say a few things about Amos? The two of you spent many a day together on your adventures."

He looked down at his feet. "I don't think I can."

"You knew him well, even better than me in some ways, I think."

"I'll try, but . . ."

"I know, honey. It's gonna be hard, but please consider it." Mary looked to Luke. "Would you get the bag of stuff I brought?"

Luke left and returned with a burlap sack.

"Put it inside," Mary said.

Luke lifted the lid on the pine casket, put the sack in, and closed the top.

"If you have anything you want to put in there, go ahead," Mary said to Brody.

Momma walked out the door onto their brand new porch. Brody and Papa had worked hard to finish it before the funeral. "It's time," she said. "Folks are here."

Chapter Twenty-One

Everyone filed out of the house, except for Mary who pulled her chair to the doorway. There were a few people Brody didn't recognize, but others he remembered as some of the sharecroppers.

Brody saw Wolf and Joseph getting off their horses. Todd had already launched himself at Papa as he came up to greet them.

A lone figure was standing at the edge of the yard. When he saw Brody, Eli walked up and offered his hand. "I'm real sorry for what my kin done to you. I'm ashamed I had a part in any of it."

Brody took his hand and shook it. "We already squared that up, Eli."

"Yep, you sure can pack a punch, farm boy," Eli chuckled.

Brody's smile turned serious. "I know your uncle forced you to do some bad things. I also know if it was not for you, they probably would have shot me the night they burned the house down."

Eli nodded and looked toward Mary just inside the doorway. "I'm not going to stay. I figure his wife would not take kindly to meeting me, knowing I was a Miller. Please give her my regards, and tell her I am sorry."

"I will."

"You take care of yourself, Brody." Eli walked away.

"You too," Brody called after him. "Maybe I'll see you around."

Brody saw a man dressed in black riding in a buggy. Papa spoke to him as the buggy came to a stop in the yard. He led the man toward the cabin, introducing him to folks as they went.

"This is Pastor Wood," he said to Brody. Just inside the door, the pastor knelt next to Mary. They spoke in hushed words, and then Mary pointed to Anna and Luke sitting in the rockers on the porch. He rose and walked out to meet them. He flipped through his Bible while they spoke.

Todd trotted over and yanked on Brody's arm. "Who is that coming?"

Brody looked to see some men riding up on horseback. Behind them was a wagon with people in the front and back. "I don't know who they are."

Someone tapped him on the shoulder. "I was told you will be speaking," the pastor said.

"I will try, sir," Brody said.

"After I'm finished," Pastor Wood said, "I will ask if there is anyone who would like to speak. That's when you come up."

"Yes, sir."

The pastor went back up on the porch and cleared his throat. His voice boomed out nice and clear. "Would everyone please gather around so you can hear me?"

As Brody moved forward, he heard more people arriving. Glancing back, he saw two older men and three women walking up to the group.

His heart gave a leap when he saw Doctor Slaughter pull his buggy into the yard. As Sarah waited for her father to help her down, she looked around. Her face lit up with a smile when she caught sight of Brody. Doc noticed and shook his head— whether in amusement or resignation, Brody wasn't sure.

Sarah moved gracefully through the people, greeting folks as she worked her way to Brody. "I'm sorry we are late," she said.

"It hasn't started yet."

"And I'm sorry you're having to go through this. I wish it hadn't happened."

Brody sighed. "Me too."

The preacher stepped to the edge of the porch. "We are gathered. . . ." He hesitated when he looked out toward the road. "Hmm. Sorry, folks, let's wait a few more minutes."

"There's more people coming," Sarah said.

Two riders arrived, and behind them four horses pulled two more wagonloads of people. Most of the men were wearing military uniforms. An older man, who was missing a leg, hobbled on wooden crutches to the edge of the gathering. His uniform was Confederate gray and had suffered harsh wear, as had the skin on his face and hands.

Leaning close to Sarah's ear, Brody whispered, "I can't believe all these people have come."

Another soldier walked over to stand next to the one-legged man. Two more men and a very short woman soon joined them.

Finally, the preacher held up his hand. "We are gathered here today to pay our final respects to a good man. I would like to open with a passage from the book of John." He opened his Bible. "Greater love hath no man than this, that a man lay down his life for his friends." He closed the Book. "That describes this man. Amos, or Ames as some knew him," he smiled over at Brody, "was born a slave, but he died a free man. I was told he had a harsh upbringing and that he survived the war, being lost on a mountain, and false accusations, but through it all he was strong in spirit and he trusted in the good Lord."

The preacher's voice rose with emotion.

"Brothers and sisters, as Amos discovered, if you let the Lord set your path, amazing works will happen. Amos regained his lost family and cleared his name of all wrongdoing. God is good, amen?"

A chorus of agreements rang out.

"And though he gained much, he gained a far greater prize than any earthly one could be offered, the day he gave up his life to save those he cared for most deeply."

Several ladies murmured, "Yes, Lord."

"He left behind his wife, Mary, and one daughter, Anna who is with child. I didn't have the pleasure of meeting this man, but Mary has told me that he was of Christian faith."

Pastor Wood opened his Bible again. "The Book tells us that a man's name is precious and his day of death is more precious than his day of birth. Today is a day to rejoice." He looked at Brody. "Is there anyone who would like to pay tribute to this man?"

Already? Brody thought. He started forward but was cut off by the short lady standing at the edge of the group. She walked up the steps and faced the crowd. Her sun-kissed cheeks puffed outward as she released a large breath.

"I'm sorry. I'm nervous." She brushed blond strands of hair, with tiny signs of gray, out of her face. "My father died when I was young, before the war. My mother did her best, but my sisters and I went to bed hungry most nights."

She looked to Mary, sitting in the doorway. "The summer of eighteen-sixty was especially hard. I don't know if we would have made it if it had not been for Amos. He risked a beating or worse just to sneak a few vegetables out of his master's garden. Every day we would walk home from school and see him standing at the edge of the field with a tomato, squash, or some okra hidden under his shirt."

Her gaze was fixed somewhere beyond the gathering of people, as if she was reliving her memories. "Those days . . . they felt like Christmas."

She started to step down but hesitated. "I just wanted his family to know that."

As soon as she was back in the crowd, one of the soldiers came up. His Confederate outfit was flawless with sharp pleats and not a wrinkle in sight. "Ames joined us under duress, and we thought of him as a coward. Some of the men, myself included, treated him in an unfriendly manner. He proved himself in Camden when he sounded the alarm and exposed a sneak attack by some dirty blue-bellies."

"We were not sneaking!" one of the Union soldiers shouted. A sharp elbow from the woman standing next to him stopped his protest. He paused and then nodded knowingly as if he understood this was not the place for an argument.

The Confederate on the porch continued. "Ames kept us from being killed or captured that day. We thought differently about him after that. He was a good man, a different sort of man, but a good one." The soldier straightened his jacket and stepped down.

Another Confederate came forward. This time it was the one-legged man, but before he could speak, a younger Union soldier joined him.

Sarah nudged Brody. "What's going on?"

"I do not know. I never expected all this," he whispered.

The older man leaned on his crutches and faced everyone. He motioned to the Union soldier at his side. "Chip and I fought each other on the Devil's Backbone. A cannonball took my leg clean off, and I lay out there with bullets flying all around. I said my last prayer that God's will be done."

He shifted his crutches and raised a hand toward the heavens. "And His will was done. Ames came through that gunfire and cinched his belt around what was left of my leg. He never said a word, even when he drug me around behind a big boulder."

The Union soldier cleared his throat. "I took a musket ball in my shoulder and one in my leg. I couldn't walk or crawl, and here come this tall black man dressed in gray. His eyes were wild, and I just knew he would finish me off, but he didn't. He grabbed me under the armpits and off we went. Ames plopped me down next to old Gus here. That's how we met, bleeding behind a big rock on the Devil's Backbone."

Gus and Chip shook hands. Chip came down from the porch, but Gus raised one of his crutches and pointed toward the crowd. "Ames taught us something. Here we were, two white men, out there killing each other over slavery! And both of us owe our lives to a man once bound by it. That will change how a person thinks."

He paused, and everyone remained dead silent. Reaching

behind him, the man pulled a rolled newspaper out of his back pocket. "I just wish I would have known he didn't die in the war." Gus squeezed the paper hard, wrinkling it in his fingers. "It's a shame the way he went, by the hand of that criminal. Just a dadburn shame."

Chip helped him down the steps. When no one else came forward, Brody's heart thumped faster.

The preacher motioned for him, but Brody still hesitated. How could he say anything without breaking down? All of the words spoken about Ames had brought him to the very edge of an emotional cliff. He walked to the porch, went up, and stood next to one of the posts. Placing a hand on it, he steadied himself on weak legs.

"I . . . I'm . . . Well, I'm Brody Martin. Me and Ames spent a lot of time together." Brody's throat burned. He swallowed hard and wiped his forehead on his sleeve. "Ames thought he was a coward. I don't know why, but he did."

He glanced at Sarah and then looked at Momma and Papa. "The man I knew wasn't a coward . . . far from it. And it sounds like many of you know it too, but sometimes . . . Well, sometimes people don't know what they are. Maybe you think you are nothing. Maybe you feel like a coward sometimes."

A tear left his eye, tickling the side of his face as it trailed down. "But maybe you are somebody's hero. You could be. Ames wasn't a coward. I mean, the stories we just heard . . ."

Brody strained to keep from crying. A few more tears formed in his eyes but he stared ahead, fighting to continue. "Ames saved me from a hunting accident." Brody gave a nervous chuckle. "And a panther."

The short woman in the front had been crying, but now she laughed.

"And a bear." He smiled and redirected his misery into the humor of how many times Ames had come to his aid. "And a wildman in Indian Territory."

Several people were smiling and nodding.

"And he saved me from the Millers more than once." Everyone's smiles disappeared at the mentioning of the Millers. Brody took a deep breath while trying to decide the final words to speak of Ames at his funeral.

Finally, a perfect send-off came to mind. "If there is such a thing as a guardian angel, I think mine was tall, black, and walked with a limp." He cleared his throat. "And I'm going to miss him."

He stepped down.

People clapped. Most of the women—and even some of the men—were crying.

Later, after the food was gone and things had settled down, everyone formed a line, some on horseback, some in wagons, and others on foot. The casket, filled with memories of a great man, was loaded into a wagon.

The procession moved toward Fort Smith and stopped at Oak Cemetery. A coffin-sized hole had been dug already, the dirt mounded neatly beside it. Several ropes were stretched across the hole and tied off.

Brody, Luke, Papa, Joseph, Chip, and one of the Confederate soldiers helped carry the casket and place it on the ropes. Men on either side untied them and lowered the wooden box.

Watching the casket going into the hole was hard for Brody. Ames wasn't inside. His body was out there along the river somewhere. Brody felt it wasn't right for his eternal resting place to be unknown.

"I'm going to find him," he whispered to Sarah. "I'll keep looking 'til I do."

After the burial, everyone gave their condolences to Mary, Anna, Luke, and Brody before heading out. Brody spent a bit more time with the folks who had traveled so far to tell their stories about Ames and learned even more that made him appreciate his friend.

Back home, Momma sat next to Papa at the table. She hugged him and let out an exhausted sigh. "That was the best funeral I believe I have ever been to."

"Uh huh," Papa agreed, leaning over to kiss her on the forehead.

A restlessness coursed over Brody, making him fidget. "I think Buck needs to stretch his legs a bit. Might ride him to the back of the property and look for Todd's treasure again."

Momma said, "Papa can go with you."

Looking from Momma and back to Papa, Brody said, "If you don't mind, Buck can be my company."

Papa said, "That will be fine, son. I need to get started on a new bed for Momma, so we can get off the hard floor. We'll see you in a little while."

Brody went outside and immediately rubbed both hands through his hair. The urge to get away overwhelmed him. He had bottled his emotions all day long, and the effort had taken its toll. He went behind the new house, saddled Buck, and then walked the horse around front.

As he passed the remains of the burnt house, he noticed something glinting in the sunlight. He dropped Buck's reins and moved closer. He stopped still when he saw what it was.

Lying on the charred bottom porch step was a shiny gold piece, a double eagle.

Chapter Twenty-Two

The coin sparkled as the sunlight glinted across its surface. Brody's first intention was to pick it up, but he didn't. He stared. He thought. His mind raced over all the possibilities of how the coin could have found its way there.

He and Ames had talked there. He remembered them discussing how everything had worked out. He remembered Ames showing him the gold eagle he believed was bringing him good luck.

Brody bent at the waist and reached for it but stopped short. His fingertips hovered above the gold eagle before he withdrew his hand and walked away. After a few steps, he twisted around and sat in the grass, facing the burnt steps. He stared at the coin, struggling with its meaning.

Is he alive?

Had Ames survived and left the coin for him to find? Or had he dropped it on the day of the house-raising? Brody rubbed his face and pictured Ames tossing the eagle into the air. He clearly saw him catching it and placing the gold eagle in his pocket.

Getting to his feet, Brody went back to the steps and collected the gold piece. It was clean and cold in his palm. He turned it over and over in his hand, searching for any clue that it belonged to Ames.

What if?

He wondered if someone from the funeral could have dropped it. There were people everywhere. Someone could have wandered over to the burnt house. Brody held the coin over the steps and dropped it. The heavy gold piece thumped hard against the wood, flipped in the air, and landed with a muffled *ching*.

They would have heard that. Wouldn't they?

With all his heart, he wanted to believe Ames had left it for him to find. But if he did, why? He remembered all the times he caught Ames staring out toward the mountains. Brody looked at the steps. *Right there. You sat right there and told me you weren't fit for being around folks.*

Studying the ground around the steps, Brody found part of a single boot print. The dirt was dry and hard to the touch. The track had clearly been made while the ground was wet.

Brody's hand began to shake as he put the coin in his pocket. The ground had been dry when he and Ames had talked at the old steps. It rained that night, and Ames left the next morning— the morning Frank shot him.

Ames didn't sleep much that night. He could have been outside before everyone else and might have left the coin then.

Brody went to Buck, climbed on the saddle, but didn't ride away. His gaze went back to the steps and the boot track again. It had rained the evening he went out looking for Ames. It had rained hard, one of the worst storms he had ever seen. He stopped breathing for a few seconds. *Surely that track would have been washed away.*

Prickly chills danced across his skin. He kicked Buck into a run, cutting across the prairie. As Buck's hooves pounded the earth, the wind roared in Brody's ears while his heart raced in his chest.

He laughed, a loud hearty laugh, one that released all of his tension and sadness. Deep inside he acknowledged the chance he could be wrong, but for now, in this most important moment, he chose to believe Ames was alive!

Brody slowed Buck to a trot. He wrapped the reins around the horn, raised his hands into the air, and shouted for joy. He shouted for hope, and yelled so loud he thought God could surely hear him.

Epilogue

Months passed, and he remained silent about the gold coin. Telling everyone he thought Ames might be alive would do no good. If it was true, Ames had made the decision to go back to the mountains. It would be nearly impossible to find him.

One evening, Brody packed a picnic and took Sarah to a section of rolling hills near his house. They ate, talked, and laughed. Brody was finally living a happy life again.

While Sarah was wrapping everything in the picnic blanket, he walked to a part of the hill where he could see some mountains in the distance.

Ames was out there somewhere, maybe on the Devil's Backbone, maybe in some beautiful valley. He was out there, but Brody felt him all around. The trees, the creeks, the smell of the woods—it all reminded him of Ames, especially the wind. Brody stood alone on the hill and heard God's breath blowing the leaves and swaying giant oak limbs. Emotion swelled inside him. Ames was home again.

Sarah came up the hill and took his hand in hers.

Brody cleared his throat. "You know, Sarah, sometimes the winds brings nothing but a breeze, but sometimes . . . sometimes it brings hope."

Todd's Treasure
Is Out There!

Brody and Todd hid the treasure box in 1881 and it was never found. It's still where they left it, and if you are the first to find it, you can keep Todd's Treasure! You can use clues in this series of books (*The Devil's Backbone*, *The Devil's Trap*, and *The Devil's Den*) to get you there.

You will have to read carefully to discover everything you'll need. Just remember that it's been at least 136 years since the box was hidden. The landscape will have changed greatly. The trees will have grown, and so has Fort Smith.

Please read how Brody hid the box. It is not buried. You will not need a shovel. Please do not dig any holes. Use a compass and your brain and go for it.

Before you head out, be sure to check James's blog at JamesBabb.wordpress.com. If you find Todd's Treasure, the items inside are yours to keep, but leave the box for others to find. Please follow directions on the blog and send a photo of yourself at the site. James will ship an autographed book to the first person to find Todd's Treasure!

If you check the blog and see that the treasure has already been found, feel free to go on the hunt anyway. Leave a note in the box, or anything you wish. Send a photo, proving you found Todd's Treasure, and your picture will be placed on James's website and he will send you an autographed bookmark.

Happy hunting!

Devil's Den facts . . .

Buffalo. The buffalo were a huge part of native American lives, especially the Sioux, Cheyenne, Comanche, and Blackfoot. The importance of the buffalo spread to all tribes, especially after the relocation in the 1830s. Extreme over-hunting by men and disease from cattle diminished buffalo populations from multimillions to nearly nothing in the 1880s. "Massive hunting parties arrived by train, with thousands of men packing .50 caliber rifles, and leaving a trail of buffalo carnage in their wake. The railroads began to advertise excursions for hunting by rail, where trains encountered massive herds alongside the tracks. Hundreds of men aboard the trains climbed to the roofs and took aim, or fired from their windows, leaving countless 1,500-pound animals where they died" (Smithsonian.com, *Harper's Weekly*).

Cherokee language. Wolf's and Joseph's conversations sounded strange to Brody's ears. In 1821, George Guess, or Gist (Sequoyah), developed a written Cherokee language. It was called a syllabary, and it took him twelve years to complete it. Words that Brody heard include **atsutsa** (*boy*, sounds like I-Chew-A-Jaw), **tla** (*no*, sounds like Claw), **unalii** (*friend*, sounds like You-Gnaw-Lee), and **waya** (*wolf*, sounds like Why-Ha). Search YouTube for "Cherokee Word of the Week" to hear and see Cherokee words. Also go to VisitCherokeeNation.com to learn more about these great people and their history.

The Devil's Backbone. This is a long ridge located south of Fort Smith, near Greenwood, Arkansas. The Union and

Confederates fought a battle on the ridge, in the edges of Indian Territory, on September 1, 1863.

Devil's Den State Park. North of Crawford County, you will find Washington County and The Devil's Den. Located high in the Ozark Mountains, it's a good place to escape the heat of the lowlands in the summer. There are many nooks, crannies, and caves. The Devil's Den cave and The Devil's Icebox are located close together. These are the two caves that Brody visited. There are many theories as to how the area got its name. According to Ernie Deane (author of the book *Arkansas Place Names*), Devil's Den got its name when early settlers exploring nearby caves reported hearing sounds that they described as the roaring of the devil.

Fort Smith Jail. In 1881, the jail at Fort Smith, Arkansas, was located in the basement under the courthouse. The conditions that were described to Brody were accurate, if not worse. In May 1881, the *Arkansas Traveler* reported that more than 100 prisoners were incarcerated there. During the summer of 1888, there were 109 prisoners in the jail. A woman named Anna Dawes visited the jail with her father, Senator Henry Dawes. She wrote an article describing the conditions, saying, "It is a veritable hell on earth." A single chamber pot was located in the fireplace in the hope that the smell would rise up the chimney. Men convicted of all sorts of crimes were thrown in together. Anna Dawes closed her article by saying, "What excuse has the government of the United States to offer for the existence and continuance of this scandal?" Many believe that her article greased the government's budget wheels and allowed for the construction of a new jail a few years later.

Locusts. The locust is a swarming species of short-horned grasshopper. Locusts swarmed parts of Arkansas in 1881. The *Arkansas Gazette* reported insect swarms numbering in the millions on May 7, 1881. While these swarms could do major damage, they were far from the largest ever recorded. Seven years before, in 1874, 120 billion locusts swarmed the Midwest in one of the worst plagues in modern times. "The locusts scoured the fields of crops, the trees of leaves, every blade of grass, the wool off the sheep, the harnesses off horses, the paint off wagons, and the handles off pitchforks." Read this wonderful article and collection of information titled, "1874: The Year of the Locust," at HistoryNet.com by Chuck Lyons.

Lynching. Lynching was the practice of punishing people, guilty or not, without due process of law, usually by hanging at the hands of angry citizens. In 1881, the *Arkansas Gazette* reported many instances of angry mobs taking justice into their own hands. Those lynched included WRL Brad (January 7), Shary O'Neal (January 20), Henry Smith (July 13), JF Bruce (September 13), John Taylor (September 13), Jim Cunningham (October 20), Charles Jones Lynch (November 1), and James Holland (November 29). In 1892, 241 persons were lynched in the United States. The top three states were Louisiana (29), Tennessee (28), and Arkansas (25) (*Chicago Tribune,* January 1892). From 1882 to 1968, 4,743 persons were lynched in the United States, although not all lynchings were recorded. Seventy-nine percent of them took place in the South.

Bass Reeves. Marshal Reeves is a real historical figure. He was possibly the first black U.S. Marshal (1875). Bass Reeves served as a marshal for thirty-two years. The famous Belle

Starr surrendered to him. He also arrested his own son, Benjamin, for murder. Bass Reeves was born a slave in Crawford County in 1838. During the Civil War, Reeves fled into Indian Territory and lived with Indians. During his career he was shot at many times but never wounded. He often used disguises or portrayed himself as something other than a lawman in order to make an arrest. He killed fourteen outlaws in the line of duty and arrested 3,000. You can see a bronze statue of him at Pendergraft Park in Fort Smith, Arkansas.

Sharecroppers. Some landowners in the south used sharecropping as nothing more than a legal form of slavery of people of all color. They were known to alter the figures and contracts in a way that would never allow their sharecroppers to climb out of debt.

Trail of Tears. The Indian Removal Act was created in 1830 during Andrew Jackson's presidency. The act allowed the relocation of five Indian tribes—Choctaw, Seminole, Creek, Chickasaw, and Cherokee—by force. All five tribes were marched through Arkansas. The Cherokee were the last to give up the fight to stay on their lands. They fought a long, hard battle in the courts and otherwise, but were relocated in 1838–1839. Indians were so opposed to any help from the men evicting them that many refused to use the ferries for river crossing and instead waded or swam across. Hundreds of members of each tribe died from the elements and disease on the long trip to Indian Territory, which was eventually reduced in size and later became the state of Oklahoma. The removal of the five tribes became known as the Trail of Tears. You can find information and maps of the Arkansas Trail of Tears routes at ArkansasHeritageTrails.com.

Wampum. Practicing an old tradition, Wolf gave Brody wampum beads. Wampum was made from the quahog clam, and the beaded belts represented peace, trade, and treaties. They were given at important meetings and during visits to other groups or tribes.

The Wildman of Indian Territory. The killer Brody and Ames fought in *The Devil's Trap* was based on a real event in history. While it's unknown when the man started killing, his first verified victim was in 1883, which means he must have survived his encounter with Brody in 1881! Read the amazing, true story of "The Panther" and about some of his sixteen victims at JamesBabb.wordpress.com, or TheOsageTerror.blogspot.com, where you will find links to newspapers articles from the 1800s.

Wolves. Encounters with wolves were on the rise in 1881. In the *Arkansas Gazette,* there were many reports in these issues: "Wolves in Lee County" (March 17, 1881), "Wolves in Drew County" (June 1, 1881), and "Izard County Wolf Attack" (July 12, 1881).

Acknowledgments

One of my biggest fans was my father. He was a man of few words but fell in love with *The Devil's Backbone* and asked me very often when the next book would be finished. When *The Devil's Trap* came out, he stayed up into the night to finish it and was anxious for *The Devil's Den*. I wish I could have written faster—oh, how I wish that. Well, it's finished, and I wish with all my heart he could be here to read it. I can only hope Heaven has a library.

I'd like to thank my family and friends for all of their help.

My readers have kept me writing, and I appreciate every one of you. I am continually amazed at the number of Brody's fans.

The Fort Smith Museum and Library were a tremendous help with the research, and special thanks go out to Terry Elder and Tim Scott for all their help at Devil's Den State Park.

JAMES BABB's first historical adventure novel, *The Devil's Backbone,* won an IPPY Award in juvenile fiction and was also selected by the Arkansas Historical Association as a winner of the Susannah DeBlack Award awarded to books for young readers. The sequel, *The Devil's Trap,* received recognition, along with *The Devil's Backbone,* at the Next Generation Indie Book Awards. A self-confessed "reluctant reader" in adolescence, Babb writes for those same readers, who have embraced his vivid characters and taut narrative style. He lives with his wife, Suzanne, in De Queen, Arkansas.